TEMPTED BY DR DAISY

BY
CAROLINE ANDERSON

First published in Great Britain 2011
by Mills & Boon, an imprint of Harlequin (UK) Limited.
Large Print edition 2012
Harlequin (UK) Limited, Eton House,
18-24 Paradise Road, Richmond, Surrey TW9 1SR

© Caroline Anderson 2011

ISBN: 978 0 263 22442 9

Harlequin (UK) policy is to use papers that are natural, renewable and recyclable products and made from wood grown in sustainable forests. The logging and manufacturing process conform to the legal environmental regulations of the country of origin.

Printed and bound in Great Britain
by CPI Antony Rowe, Chippenham, Wiltshire

LP

Dear Reader,

When I was asked to write a duet of two closely linked books, I thought 'How close can people be?' And the answer? Identical twins who are both gorgeous guys and amazing doctors—my LEGENDARY WALKER DOCTORS. But they're not just normal twins, but twins who'd shared the same amniotic sac, who'd been in touch with each other from the first moment and who now, 34 years later, were still very close emotionally and in their working lives. You really can't get closer than that—and for both Ben and Matt, their journeys have been paved with tragedy and pain.

But then Ben moves to Yoxburgh, where Daisy and Amy, dear friends and colleagues, are waiting in the wings.

Ben has a daughter, little Florence, who is the centre of his world—until he meets Daisy. He just has to find a way for both of them to trust again, so together they can give Florence the family they all long for in TEMPTED BY DR DAISY.

For Matt and Amy, the past is so painful they can't bear to go there again, but when Ben and Daisy fall in love, her best friend and his twin are brought together again and circumstances conspire to force them to face their past and deal with the loss that drove them apart in THE FIANCÉE HE CAN'T FORGET.

Writing their stories was heart-wrenching but wonderful, and I hope you enjoy reading them as much as I enjoyed coaxing them along each step of the way.

With love,

Caroline

Caroline Anderson has the mind of a butterfly. She's been a nurse, a secretary, a teacher, run her own soft-furnishing business, and now she's settled on writing. She says, 'I was looking for that elusive something. I finally realised it was variety, and now I have it in abundance. Every book brings new horizons and new friends, and in between books I have learned to be a juggler. My teacher husband John and I have two beautiful and talented daughters, Sarah and Hannah, umpteen pets, and several acres of Suffolk that nature tries to reclaim every time we turn our backs!' Caroline also writes for Mills & Boon® Cherish™.

Recent titles by the same author:

Medical™ Romance
ST PIRAN'S: WEDDING OF THE YEAR
THE SURGEON'S MIRACLE
THE VALTIERI MARRIAGE DEAL

Mills & Boon® Cherish™
THE BABY SWAP MIRACLE
MOTHER OF THE BRIDE

**Did you know these are also available as eBooks?
Visit www.millsandboon.co.uk**

CHAPTER ONE

SHE could hear water running.

Her new neighbour, whoever he might be, was up and about already. Well, she hoped he'd slept better than she had, she thought grumpily. He'd kept her awake until midnight moving things, and the cat deciding she was hungry at five thirty *really* didn't help.

To be fair, he hadn't been that noisy, but she wasn't feeling fair after *another* hen weekend, and *another* of her friends settling down to matrimonial bliss. That left her and Amy, but she couldn't see Amy letting anyone close, and as for her—well, where *were* all the decent single men without a ton of emotional baggage? Not in Yoxburgh, that was for sure, and even if they were, she wasn't sure she was quite ready to dip her toe in that particular pond again.

She fed Tabitha, made herself a cup of tea and went out to the conservatory. Dawn was breaking, the sky washed pale pink above the rooftops to the east, and she curled up on a chair overlooking her pretty little garden, pressed the mental 'reset' button and let herself come to slowly.

It was her favourite time of the day, before the rest of the world got up, and she cradled her mug in her hands, snuggled further down into the chair and listened to the sounds of the glorious spring morning.

The birds were singing, and she could hear boards creaking next door, more of those masculine footsteps running down the stairs, a muffled exclamation—and an almighty crash that sent Tabitha fleeing for the hills and made Daisy spill her tea.

'Oops!' she murmured, trying to tune out the man's voice as she blotted uselessly at her dressing gown, but it was hard to ignore. What on *earth* had he done? Something pretty drastic, judging by the expletives seeping through the thin party wall.

And then there was silence.

'Are you OK?' she called warily—although she didn't really need to raise her voice.

'Um—yeah. Sort of,' he replied, his voice muffled by the wall. 'Sorry. Minor crisis.'

'Anything I can do?'

A despairing laugh, then, 'Not unless you're a plumber.'

She heard footsteps striding down the hall, then a door opening, and a knock at her front door.

She opened it, and her mouth sagged. Wow, he was...

Well, he was many things. Tall. Broad. Gorgeous. Young enough to be interesting, old enough to have something about him. And there was *plenty* about him. He was covered in filthy, sodden debris, his suit drenched and splattered, his hair full of bits of stuff, his once-white shirt a dirty, streaky grey. In the striking, really rather fabulous blue eyes lurked a hint of irony that made her smile.

Then the eyes tracked down her dressing gown and stopped on the huge tea-stain. 'What happened to you?' he asked incredulously, and she gave a stunned little laugh.

'I thought that was my line,' she said, trying not to laugh any more because it really, really wasn't funny, but his mouth quirked.

'Ah. My ceiling came down,' he explained unnecessarily, and Daisy had to bite her lip. To her surprise his eyes creased in a smile.

'Sorry about the noise. And the language. I'm Ben, by the way,' he said, holding out his hand, then withdrawing it and wiping it on his trousers, scanning it before offering it again. She took it, noting that as well as being a little wet and gritty, it was warm and firm. Strong.

And his voice—a hint of something that could have been Yorkshire? A little gruff. A little blunt. And a *lot* sexy.

'Daisy,' she said, and let herself smile properly. 'Welcome to Rivenhall Villas. May it get better.'

He gave a slightly desperate laugh and closed his eyes, dragging his hand over his face and smearing the dirt into it. A streak of blood joined the dirt, welling slowly from a thin cut over his eyebrow.

'I can only hope. I don't suppose you know a plumber?'

She tightened the belt of her saturated dressing gown, hopped over the low fence between the diamond-patterned paths and peered down his hall at a scene of utter devastation. His kitchen had disappeared under a sea of sodden lime plaster and broken laths, and there was a slow, steady drip from a dangling lump of ceiling. The rush, she sensed, was over, but...

'Just a plumber?' she murmured thoughtfully, and behind her she heard another wry laugh.

'A plumber would be a pretty good start. An electrician might be a handy second, that light's hanging at a jaunty angle. And a plasterer, perhaps?'

'Mmm. It seems to have stopped, though.'

'Yeah. I reckon it was the waste. I'd just had a bath.'

'Ah. Very likely, then. I tell you what,' she said, turning back to him and finding him right behind her. She took a step back, and a nice deep breath, because under the plaster filth and the wet dog smell coming off his suit was the lingering remains of some seriously interesting aftershave. Citrusy, with a touch of amber...

'You were about to tell me something,' he prompted, and she collected herself.

'Um—yes. Why don't I throw on some clothes and come and help you clear up? I've got an hour before I have to leave for work.' And a nice long shower planned, but she could feel that going out of the window rapidly.

'Lucky you. I have to leave now. Let's face it, it can't get any worse, but I can't do anything about it and I've got bigger fish to fry. It's my first day in a new job, I don't have another suit or any way of getting the filth out of my hair, and there's no way I'm turning a tap on! I guess I'll just have to make do with spitting on a handkerchief.'

Obviously he hadn't looked in a mirror yet.

'This is going to take more than spitting on a hankie to sort out,' she said drily. 'And you've got a cut over your left eye. Do you have another shirt?'

He fingered his eyebrow gingerly and nodded. 'And trousers and a jacket, but not the power suit, sadly.'

'Can't help you there,' she said, giving up all hope of starting her day with any kind of normality. 'However, I do have a shower. Why don't you grab some clean stuff and sort yourself out while I find you a plumber?'

'Really?'

'Really. Find your clothes, I'll get dressed and

I can make a start on the clean-up, too. I have a vacuum that's very good for sucking up spills.'

'Spills?' He choked on a laugh, and the smile that crinkled his eyes made her stomach turn over. 'There's a bathful of water on that floor.'

'No problem. It can cope. I'll just have to empty it lots—if I can find the sink.'

He frowned. 'Daisy, are you sure? It's a hell of an imposition.'

Well, at least he realised it. Her morning was running away with her, but she couldn't just leave him like this. She found a smile—not as hard as she'd thought, because those eyes were really quite...

'I thought you were in a hurry?' she said, and squeezed past him, hopped over the fence and ran upstairs, dragged on her gardening clothes, put a towel in the bathroom for him and had just hauled the vacuum up from the cellar as he appeared at her door.

'Look, you really don't have to clean up—'

'Don't be silly, it's nothing. Bathroom's at the top of the stairs, straight ahead of you. I've put you out a towel on the side of the bath and the plumber's calling me back.'

He didn't believe it.

He should. Things like this seemed to happen to him these days. He tipped his head forwards so it was under the stream of hot water and let out a tired, frustrated sigh. He'd known moving into the house before it was fixed was rash, but—this rash?

Thank God for Daisy. The shower was bliss. He could have stood there all day under the streaming hot water, but he didn't have time. He borrowed some of her shampoo and washed the filth out of his hair, and discovered some interesting lumps and bumps on his scalp. The cut over his eyebrow was stinging, too. Damn. He sluiced the grit and grime off his body, gave himself a very hasty rub-down with Daisy's borrowed towel, then dressed in record time, scowled at the cut on his eyebrow, frowned at a mark on his shoes that wouldn't shift and gave up.

There was nothing more he could do. Nothing he had time to do. His ruined suit was lying in a soggy heap in the bottom of Daisy's pristine and rather beautiful bath, and he left it there. He'd sort everything out with her later, once he'd got today out of the way.

He could hear the vacuum going next door, sucking up the water. Bless her heart. Of all the days—and of all the neighbours, he thought with a bemused smile. What a star.

A small black cat with huge ears and brilliant green eyes watched him disdainfully through the banisters as he went downstairs. He stretched out a hand to her, and after a second she turned away, and he carried on down with a wry chuckle, dismissed.

He hopped over the pointless but decorative little fence and went into his house, to find Daisy in the middle of the kitchen somehow bringing order to the chaos. The water was largely gone, and she was shoving debris to the side with a broom.

'Daisy, you don't have to do that! I'll clear it up later.'

'I'm nearly done. I've cleared the rubble off the boxes to give them a chance to dry out. I think you might have lost some crockery or glasses—that one tinkled a bit.'

He shrugged. Glasses he could live without. At least he was alive. He fingered the cut again, and she peered at it.

'You need a plaster on that.'

He shrugged again. 'No idea where they are, but I'm sure I'll live. I don't suppose you've heard from the plumber, have you?'

'No, not yet. Take my mobile number and give me a missed call, and I'll send you a text when I hear from him.'

He keyed it in, then slid the phone back into his pocket and ran a hand through his damp hair. 'Look, I'm sorry, I've left my suit in your bath, but I have to go now. I'll deal with it later, and all of this. You don't have to do any more—'

'Go. I'm nearly done. I'll see you later. Can I just drop the door shut on the latch?'

'That's fine. Thank you so much. I owe you, big-time.'

'Too right. I'll expect a slap-up dinner at the least,' she said drily, swiping an armful of soggy plaster rubble off the worktop onto the filthy floor.

'Consider it done.'

She flashed a smile at him, a streak of dirt on her cheek giving her the impish, mischievous look of a little girl having way too much fun—and he didn't really want to start thinking about

Daisy having fun, because it was a long, long time since he'd had fun with a woman, and for all she might look fleetingly like the little girl she'd once been, there was nothing but woman under those clothes. And he was taking her out to dinner?

He cleared his throat, nodded curtly and went. 'Phew.'

Daisy straightened up, blew the hair back out of her eyes and looked around. Utter chaos, but at least it was organised chaos now. The rubble was swept into a heap, the boxes had been blotted dry and the water sucked up—and she was going to be late for work, today of all days!

She fled, grabbing the quickest shower on record and dragging on her clothes. Her hair would have to do, she decided, pulling it back and doubling it into a loose bun in an elastic band. No time for makeup. No time for anything, and the new consultant was starting today.

Great start, she thought. Please God he wasn't an arrogant snob—or a tedious box-ticker. One of them on the team was more than enough. She ran to the car, paused in the street to shut her garden gates and headed for the hospital.

On the way she took a call from the plumber, then dropped Ben's suit into the cleaners in the hospital reception area, instructing them to be careful. She'd seen the label, and it had made her wince.

Then she legged it for the ward.

By the time she got there, people were clustered around the nursing station. She could see a man's head slightly above the rest, hear a quiet voice giving some kind of team-leading chat, and her heart sank. Damn. He was here already, doing the meet and greet. So much for making a good impression.

Evan Jones, the specialist registrar, gave the ward clock a pointed look as she squeezed into the group.

'Sorry I'm—' she began a little breathlessly, and then stopped in her tracks as the man turned and met her eyes, and if she hadn't been so busy staring at him in shock she would have missed the quickly masked flicker of surprise.

'Mr Walker, this is Dr Fuller,' Evan said, sounding and looking unimpressed, but Ben's professional smile did something utterly different in his eyes, and he brushed Evan smoothly aside.

'Yes, we've met. Dr Fuller's very kindly been doing something for me,' he explained, cutting him off at the knees, and then turned back to her. 'Any joy?'

Still shocked, running on autopilot and ready to fall in love with him for saving her from another tedious lecture, she nodded. 'Yes, it's sorted,' she told him without missing a beat. He'd found a plaster, she thought, staring at the cut above his eyebrow, but apart from that you'd never know how his day had started. He looked cool, calm and in control—more than she was.

'Thank you. I don't think you've missed much,' he said with a wry smile, then he looked back at the group. 'As I was saying, I'm looking forward to working with you all, and I hope you'll forgive me when I ask silly, irritating questions and don't know where things are or how they're done here. I'll do my best to make this transition as painless as possible, if you'll just bear with me, and if you've got anything you want to talk about, my door's always open, so to speak.'

He smiled at them all. 'Right, that's it, everybody. I know you've all got plenty to do, so I won't hold you up. Dr Jones, rather than keep you from our patients any longer, why don't I get Dr Fuller to show me round? I need to speak to her anyway, so she might as well give me a quick tour and I'll introduce myself to her properly, then I suggest we meet for coffee at nine thirty, if that's all right, and you can fill me in on anything she might have missed and show me the department in detail. Any problems with that, either of you?'

Evan looked a bit startled, but conceded with a stiff little nod. 'No, you go ahead, Mr Walker. I'm sure Dr Fuller can tell you everything you need to know. I don't really have time, anyway. There are some patients I need to see urgently.'

'Clare Griffiths,' she said, worrying about her as she had been all weekend. 'How's she doing?'

'I've seen her already. Don't worry, I can manage without you,' he said dismissively, and Ben frowned. He didn't like the sound of that at all. In fact, he was beginning not to like Evan Jones…

'Fine. We'll catch up with you later,' he said, and without pausing for breath, he ushered Daisy towards the doors.

'Doing something for you?' she muttered under

her breath, and his laugh, low and soft and in-audible except to her whispered over her nerve endings and made her shiver.

She gulped as he swiped his ID over the sensor and pushed the door open for her.

'Well, you were, it wasn't a lie. OK, first things first. I want you to fill me in on everything there is to know about the department and its politics— starting with the location of the nearest decent coffee.' His mouth tipped into a wry grin. 'Break-fast was unexpectedly cancelled.'

She had a vision of him covered in his ceil-ing, and grinned back. 'Indeed. Full English, Mr Walker, or would you rather have something sweet and sinful?'

His eyes flared slightly, and for a second her breath hitched in her throat. 'Oh, I think sweet and sinful sounds rather promising, Dr Daisy, don't you?' he murmured, and followed her out of the ward while she tried to remember how to breathe.

'So—the plumber's coming at seven?' Ben said as they sat down with huge mugs of coffee and wickedly sticky buns—sweet and sinful, she'd said, and he had to try very, very hard to keep his thoughts on track as he watched her bite into hers. 'Is that seven today or in three years' time?'

'No, today,' she said with a laugh, taking down her hair and twisting it back up again into a knot. Pity. He preferred it down. It looked soft, silky, and he could almost imagine sifting the long, dark strands through his fingers—

He stirred his coffee for something safe to do with his hands and dragged his mind back in line again. 'So how come he's available this quickly? Usually if a tradesman's any good, you have to wait weeks. Do you know him?'

She nodded. 'Yes. He's doing it as a favour to me, and he is good. He refitted my bathroom for me.'

'Ah. Yes. Your lovely bathroom. I'm afraid I left it in a horrendous mess.'

'Don't worry, it's fine, I'll deal with it later.'

'So did he charge a fortune, or did your landlord pay?'

'Landlord? I don't have a landlord,' she said ruefully. 'It's my house, and he was very reasonable, as plumbers go.'

'You're buying it alone?' he added, fishing, although it was none of his business and utterly irrelevant, he told himself firmly. He was *not* interested.

She nodded and pulled a face. 'Although sometimes I wonder how I got myself in this situation. I must be mad. I wanted my own house because I was fed up with unscrupulous landlords but I'm not quite convinced I'm really grown up enough!'

Oh, he was sure she was. She was certainly grown up enough to satisfy his frankly adolescent fantasies, he thought. She was biting into the sticky bun again and it was giving him heart failure watching her lick her lips.

And they were colleagues *and* neighbours? Sheesh, he thought, and was hauling his mind back to work when she spoke again.

'So how about you?' she asked, her clear green eyes studying him curiously. 'I mean, you're a consultant, so clearly you're old enough to have a house, but—well, without being rude, what's a consultant doing buying a run-down little semi in a place like Yoxburgh?'

Good question—and one he had no intention of answering, but at least it had dragged his mind out of the gutter. 'What's wrong with Yoxburgh?'

She shrugged. 'Nothing. I love it. It's got the

best of both worlds—good hospital, nice community, the sea, the countryside—it's a lovely town.'

'Exactly. So why should I be flawed for wanting to be here?' he asked, curious himself and trying to divert attention back to her and off his personal life.

'Oh, no reason. It's not Yoxburgh, really. It was just—I would have expected you to have a better house. Bigger. More in keeping…' She trailed to a halt, as if she felt she'd overstepped the mark—which she probably had, but she'd rescued him before six o'clock in the morning without batting an eyelid, lent him her shower, cleared up his mess, got him a plumber…

'I'm divorced,' he admitted softly, surprising himself that he was giving so much away to her, and yet oddly knowing it was safe to do so. 'And it might be modest, but the house suits my needs perfectly—or it will, when the plumber's been and I've thrown a whole lot of money at it. Besides, maybe I don't want to live in anything flashy and ostentatious—more "in keeping",' he added, making little air quotes with his fingers.

She coloured slightly, her thoughts chasing each

other transparently through her eyes, and he had to stifle a smile as she gathered herself up and sucked in a breath.

'Sorry. None of my business,' she said hastily. 'And talking of suits, I dropped yours into the dry cleaners in the main reception on the way in, and it'll be ready at five—and before you panic, I told them to take good care of it.'

'Chasing brownie points, Daisy?' he murmured, and she laughed.

'Hardly. I didn't know who you were then. I'm just a nice person.'

'You are, aren't you?'

'Not that nice. I've still got my eye on dinner,' she said with a teasing grin that diverted the blood from his brain, and he wondered how the hell he was going to keep this sudden and unwanted attraction in its box.

With huge difficulty. Damn.

He turned his attention back to his coffee, and then she said quietly, 'Thanks for covering for me so smoothly, by the way. Evan's a stickler for punctuality, and he was getting all ready to flay me later.'

'It was the least I could do. I was hardly going

to throw you to the wolves for bailing me out—literally! And Evan doesn't strike me as the friendliest of characters. He was pretty dismissive when you asked about that patient.'

A flicker of what could have been worry showed in her eyes. 'Oh, he's OK really. He can come over as a patronising jerk, but he's a good doctor. He's just a bit miffed that you got the job, I think. He was advised to apply for it, and I reckon he thought it was a shoo-in.'

'And then they had to advertise it by law, and I applied. And with all due respect to Evan, I would imagine my CV knocks spots off his.'

'Exactly. So he won't welcome you with open arms, but you should be able to rely on him.'

He gave a choked laugh. 'Well, that's good to know.'

Her mouth twitched, and those mischievous green eyes were twinkling at him again. 'So, I hope you've got some good ideas about what I was supposedly doing for you?'

He leant back in his chair and met her eyes with a twinkle of his own. 'Oh, let's say finding me some statistics on twins on the antenatal list. That should cover it. Anyway, I thought it was pretty good for a spur-of-the-moment thing. Sorry if it sounded a bit patronising, but I thought it was better than explaining I'd already had a shower in your bathroom,' he said softly, and then felt his legs disintegrate when a soft wash of colour touched her cheeks.

He cleared his throat.

'Tell me about Yoxburgh Park Hospital,' he suggested hastily, and she collected herself and gave a tiny shrug.

'It's old and new, it's on the site of the old lunatic asylum—'

'How delightfully politically incorrect,' he said drily, and she chuckled.

'Isn't it? Nearly as politically incorrect as locking up fifteen-year-old girls because their fathers or brothers had got them knocked up and if they were put away here for life then the family could pretend they'd gone mad and carry on as normal.'

'Lovely.'

'It was. It was a workhouse, really, and the pauper lunatic label was just a way of covering up what they were doing, apparently. I mean, who's going to go near a lunatic asylum? You might end up inside, and so they got away with murder, literally. But life was cheap then, wasn't it?'

'So was building, which I guess is why the old Victorian part is so magnificent.'

'Oh, absolutely, and the other plus side is that because they wanted it isolated, we've got glorious parkland all around us, tons of parking and plenty of room to expand. The locals have access to it for recreation, we have a lovely outlook—it couldn't be better, and the hospital's great. Quite a few areas of it are brand new and state of the art, like the maternity wing, and it's earning an excellent reputation. We've got a bit of everything, but it's still small enough to be friendly and it's a good place to work. Everybody knows everybody.'

'Is that necessarily a good thing?'

She gave a wry smile. 'Not always. You wait till they find out we're neighbours, for instance.'

'You think they will?'

She laughed. 'I give it three days—maybe less.'

Oh, that laugh! Musical, infectious—it was going to kill him. And then she flicked the tip of her tongue out and licked the icing off her lips, and his eyes zeroed in on them and locked.

'So—guided tour?' he suggested hastily, because if he had to sit there opposite her for very many more minutes, he was going to have to strap his hands down by his sides to stop himself reaching out and lifting that tiny smear of icing off the corner of her mouth with his fingertip.

'Sure. Where do you want to start?'

'Maternity Outpatients?' he suggested wryly. 'Then you can ask about the twins, so it's not a lie, and there's an antenatal clinic with my name on it later today, so I'm told, and it would look better if I could find it.' His eyes twinkled. 'Can't have me turning up late, clearly. Evan would have a field day with it.'

CHAPTER TWO

IT WAS a hectic day, with very little time to think about her new boss and neighbour.

She took Ben for a quick walk through the hospital—the antenatal clinic, as they'd discussed, and other key areas that he might need to visit as well as the location of the dry cleaners, and then armed with the twin statistics she took him back to the maternity unit and gave him a lightning tour of the department—the gynae, antenatal and postnatal wards, the labour ward, the theatre suite, SCBU as well, just for information, and then handed him over to Evan Jones on the dot of nine thirty and went back to the gynae ward to check her patients from last week. She had three to discharge before the afternoon antenatal clinic, then it was back to the antenatal ward and the young first-time mum with pre-eclampsia that she'd been worrying about.

Evan had said he'd already looked at her, but

she wanted to see with her own eyes, and she was glad she did. Clare wasn't looking so great. Her blood pressure was up, her feet and hands were more swollen and she was complaining of a slight headache.

Daisy had thought they should deliver her on Friday, Evan had wanted to give her longer for the sake of the baby. He'd won. And now it was looking as if it might have been the wrong thing to do.

'Right, I want you much quieter,' she told her softly, perching on the bed and taking Clare's hand. 'I guess you've had a bit of a busy weekend, and we're going to have to slow things down for you and make you rest much more. So the telly's going, the visits are down to hubby only, once a day, and I really want you to sleep, OK?'

'I can't. I'm too scared.'

'You don't need to be scared. We're taking good care of you, and all you need to do is relax, Clare. I know it's hard, but you just have to try and find that quiet place and let go, OK? Try for me?'

She nodded, rested her head back and closed her eyes.

'Good girl. We'll keep a close eye on you, and

I'm tweaking your drugs a bit, and you should feel better soon. If anything changes or you feel unwell, press the bell, and I don't want you out of bed for anything. OK?'

Clare nodded again, and Daisy left the room, closing the door silently behind her, and was re-positioning the 'Quiet, Please' sign more prominently when she became aware of someone behind her.

'Is this the woman you were concerned about?' he said softly.

'Yes—Clare Griffiths. She's got pre-eclampsia.' Daisy's voice was a quiet murmur. 'Actually, can I have a word with you about her?'

'Sure.'

They walked away from the door, and Daisy filled him in. 'I don't know if she's OK to leave. I was going to order another ultrasound. She's only 32 weeks, and Evan wants the baby to have as long as possible, so I've told her not to move a muscle, to close her eyes and rest, but it's easy to say and much harder to do, and today her hands and feet are more swollen and she's complaining of a headache. She's got a urinary catheter and we're monitoring her fluid balance.'

'Are those the notes?'

She handed him the file, and he scanned through it, and met her eyes. 'Gut feeling?'

'I think we're going to end up delivering her today.' She bit her lip. 'I wanted to do it on Friday, but Evan—'

'Evan wanted to wait. And you disagreed. He said something about that.'

She frowned. 'What?'

'Oh, just the implication that you were over-cautious.'

Daisy shrugged, disappointed that Evan had thought that rather than respecting her judgement, but maybe he'd been right. Maybe she was overreacting now. 'Do you want to examine her?'

'I thought you'd just done it?'

'I have, but—'

'But nothing. The notes tell me what I need to know. I don't want to stress her by going in straight away. If she sees me, she'll think she has to panic. And I trust you, Daisy.'

'Is that wise? You know nothing about me.'

'I know you're thorough and meticulous with the notes. Evan thought you lacked confidence.

That implies to me that you should have more confidence in your judgement, not less.'

She nodded and bit her lip. 'OK. Well, we can watch her if you're happy to. She's had steroids, the baby's as ready as it can be. I'm thinking that waiting much longer's probably not an option but I could be wrong.'

'Or you could be right. So alert Theatre, have SCBU on standby, order another ultrasound and hourly obs, and we'll give the drugs time to work and wait and see. We aren't fortune-tellers, we just have to watch and wait. Keep me up to speed.'

She nodded, and with an encouraging wink, he handed her back the notes and walked away.

There wasn't time for lunch, and she arrived at the antenatal clinic at the same time as Ben and Evan.

They were seeing the tricky patients, the mums with known problems, and she was working her way steadily through the more routine cases and trying not to think about her new neighbour and boss when her pager bleeped.

Clare Griffiths. Damn. She must have deteriorated. Handing her patient over to the clinic midwife to refer to Evan, she went straight up to the ward and found Clare looking pale and sweaty. Her face was looking more bloated, and she was clearly wretched.

As soon as she saw her, Clare started to cry.

'I'm so glad you're here. My feet really hurt, and I can't bend my fingers, my headache's worse, and I can't really see—there are flashing lights and it's as if I've got worms wriggling about all over the inside of my eyes. I'm so scared.'

Retinal haemorrhages, Daisy thought, scanning the monitor and her test results and fluid balance. The ultrasound result showed that the baby hadn't grown since the previous Thursday, and that meant it wasn't getting enough nutrition. She perched on the bed and held her hand, feeling the difference in her fingers even in two short hours. Have more confidence, Ben had said, and he trusted her. Well, let's hope I'm not overreacting now, she thought.

She rubbed her fingers soothingly. 'Don't be scared, Clare, we're looking after you,' she said, trying to inject some of that confidence into her voice, 'but I'm afraid your blood pressure's gone up again, and your blood results show your kidneys are struggling and the baby's not growing. Let me call Mr Walker and ask him to come and look at you.'

'Is this it?' she asked, sniffing and looking even more worried. 'Are you going to have to deliver me?'

'I think so,' Daisy told her honestly, and Clare swallowed.

'But it's so early—what about the baby?' she asked, welling up again.

'The baby should be all right, but if we leave it where it is it certainly won't be, and nor will you. I'm sorry, Clare, we haven't got any choice in this. I'll get Mr Walker, and I'll ring your husband and get him to come in. You might want him with you.'

She asked the midwife with them to prep her for Theatre, rang the antenatal clinic and then Clare's husband, and two minutes later Ben was in with Clare examining her. To her relief he backed her without hesitation.

'Dr Fuller's absolutely right, Clare, we need to deliver your baby now. We'll get the anaesthetist to do your epidural, and then we'll take you into Theatre. You should start to feel better almost immediately, and we have lots of babies born at this stage without any problems. We'll go and scrub, and we'll see you in Theatre in a minute. And don't worry. I know it feels scary, but it's pretty routine for us, and we'll look after you.'

His smile was kind, his manner firm and confident, and Daisy felt herself relaxing. He was right, it was routine, but Clare had every right to be scared, and he'd been good with her. Very good. It was the first time she'd seen Ben with a patient, and any reservations she might have had about their new man disappeared instantly.

'Do you feel ready to lead?' he asked Daisy as they scrubbed. 'I want that baby out fast—I think she's heading for a crisis so I don't think we should hang about. Are you up to it, or would you rather I did it this time?'

'Will you? Not because I don't think I can, but because I know you can, and it's not about pride, it's about Clare and her baby.'

He gave a gentle, understanding laugh and turned the tap off with his elbow.

'Wise words. Right, let's go.'

He was slick, and Daisy was glad she'd opted to assist rather than lead. His hands were deft and confident, and within moments, it seemed, he had their baby cradled securely in his fingers, his tiny mewling cry music to their ears.

'Hello, little one, welcome to the world,' he said softly, and then met Clare's eyes over the drapes. 'You've got a son,' he said, smiling, 'and he's looking good.'

He was—small but strong, and after a brief introduction to Clare and her flustered and emotional husband, he was whisked away to SCBU and they were able concentrate on Clare.

As much as Daisy was able to concentrate on anything except those strong, capable hands that worked so deftly, and the magnetic blue eyes that from time to time met and held her gaze over their masks for just a fraction of a second longer than necessary…

Ben made it back just in time for the plumber. He'd left Daisy settling Clare back onto the ward after he'd kept an eye on her in Recovery and then gone back to his antenatal clinic, and then she'd paged him with a message that she'd collected his suit and Clare was fine.

Brilliant.

He walked through the door, stripping off his tie and hanging his jacket on the end of the banister, and before he had time to do anything else there was a knock on the door behind him.

The man on the doorstep had a toolbox in his hand, and reassuringly grubby fingers. 'Steve, the plumber? Daisy said you'd got problems.'

The temptation to laugh hysterically nearly overwhelmed him. 'You might say that,' he offered drily, and took Steve through to the kitchen.

Daisy let herself into the house, hung up his suit, kicked off her shoes and fed the cat. She could hear Ben moving around next door, and she sat down at the table and signed the card she'd got for him in the supermarket, propped it up against the bottle of bubbly she'd also bought and ran upstairs to shower. The bath was calling her, but she was too hungry to dawdle and she wanted to know how Ben had got on with Steve.

She rubbed herself briskly dry and went back into her bedroom. Jeans? Or sweats?

Jeans, she decided, running the hairdryer over her hair and brushing it through. Jeans and a pretty top, because a girl had her pride and he'd seen her in a dressing gown covered in tea, in her gardening clothes, in her professional 'trust me, I'm a doctor' clothes, and when she popped round with his housewarming present it would be the first time she could show him who she really was.

Which was ridiculous, because she was all of those things, and in any case, why the hell did it matter what he thought of what she was wearing? He was divorced, with no doubt all sorts of emotional baggage. And he was her neighbour, and her boss. Three very good reasons why she should keep him at arm's length and have as little to do with him as possible, she reminded herself fiercely.

And washing her hair and leaving it down was all part of shedding the working day, she told herself. Shoes off, hair down, sweats on.

Except in this case it was jeans, and a pretty top, and the makeup she hadn't had time to put on first thing, because a girl had her pride.

'Oh!'

The knock on the door made her jump, and she

swiped the blob of mascara off the side of her nose and ran downstairs, pulling the door open.

He was propped against the inside of her porch, one ankle crossed over the other, hands in his pockets and wearing a pair of jeans and a cotton shirt that looked incredibly soft. She really wanted to touch it.

He smiled at her and shrugged away from the wall, and she folded her arms and propped herself up on the door frame and tried not to grin like an idiot. 'So how did you get on?' she asked.

'Fine. He was amazing. He fixed it in two minutes, he's coming on Monday to fit a new suite and he's getting me a plasterer. And an electrician's already been and fitted a temporary light, so at least I can see in the kitchen, even if I can't really use it.'

'Told you he was good. Any idea why it happened?'

'The bath trap had pulled apart. He thought the seal might have perished, but you'd think the previous owner would have found that out.'

She shook her head. 'Mrs Leggatt couldn't get upstairs. She washed in a bowl the whole time I knew her, and she never had visitors. She used the shower downstairs before that, she said.'

'Did she? Well, that doesn't work, either, which might explain the bowl.'

'Not having much luck, are you?' She shifted and smiled at him, ridiculously aware of his strong, muscled body just a foot or so away. 'I was going to come and see you later to find out how you got on. I've got your suit and a little something to try and compensate for the horrendous start. Come on in.'

He followed her, and she handed him the bottle and the card. 'It's nothing special, but I thought it might help to balance things out.' He gave a quizzical smile, and shook his head slowly. 'Ah, Daisy, I think you've done far more than a bottle of bubbly ever could. I just can't thank you enough for today,' he said softly. 'You've been amazing. Bless you.'

She felt her cheeks heat, and flashed him a quick smile before turning away and heading for the kitchen. 'It was nothing,' she said, grabbing the kettle like a lifeline and shoving it under the tap. 'You're welcome. To be honest, I'm hugely relieved you aren't a property developer or crazy

DIY-er who's going to do something awful to devalue my house! Well, at least I hope you're not.'

He chuckled. 'Well, I'll try not to, but I'm not having much luck so far! This is a lovely house, though. It gives me hope for mine.'

'They've both got most of their original features. That's really rare. I hope you're going to keep them?'

'Oh, definitely. That was one of the reasons I bought it. Luckily I'd budgeted for the kitchen and bathroom.' His mouth quirked, and she felt her heart hitch. It was ridiculous! They'd been working together all day without a problem, but here, in the intimate setting of her kitchen…

'So—how's Clare now?'

'Fine,' she said, clutching the change of topic like a lifeline. Work she could deal with. 'She's settling, her blood pressure's already coming down, her urine output's up and she's feeling a lot better. And the baby's doing well.'

'Good. For what it's worth and off the record, I would have delivered her on Friday, too, looking at the notes in more detail. Just in case she'd flared up at the weekend. She was lucky.'

She spun round, eyes wide, and stared at him. He agreed with her? 'Really?'

'Really. You were justifiably cautious.'

She felt something warm unfurling inside her, and she smiled. 'Thank you,' she said softly.

'My pleasure. Have you eaten?'

'No. I picked up a ready meal on the way home and I'm just about to cook it, but it's only enough for one or I'd offer to share. Sorry.'

'Don't worry. I was going to take you out. I owe you dinner, remember?'

She flushed again. 'Ben, I was joking.'

'Well, I wasn't, and you'd be doing me a favour. I've got no food in the house, my kitchen's destroyed and I'm starving. I haven't eaten anything today except that sticky bun, and low blood sugar makes me grumpy.'

'Oh, well, we wouldn't want you grumpy,' she said, going belly-up with a grin, and tried to tell herself she was only doing it as a favour to her boss and her pathetically easy submission was nothing to do with those gorgeous blue eyes, or the rippling muscles she'd seen as he'd pulled off his scrub top on the way through to the changing rooms after he'd delivered Clare.

Nothing to do with that at all...

They went to the bistro on the waterfront.

It had uninterrupted views of the sea, good food and it was close enough to walk to.

Not that they could see the sea, really, this late in the evening, but they could hear it as they walked along the prom, the soft rush of the waves surging up the shore, the suck on the shingle as the water receded, and they could smell it, the tang of salt sharp in the moist air.

'I love the sea,' she told him. 'I don't think I could live anywhere landlocked.'

'You want to try the Yorkshire Dales. It takes a good hour or more to get to the coast.'

'But it's worth it when you get there, surely? Doesn't Yorkshire have lovely beaches?'

'Oh, yes. Gorgeous. And Lancashire, on the west coast. It's just a bit of an expedition. London wasn't any better.'

'Is that where you've just come from?' she asked, trying not to be nosy but failing.

He grinned, his teeth flashing white in the streetlights. 'For my sins. How about you? Are you Yoxburgh born and bred?'

'No. I've only been here two years. I've got

a friend working here, and she persuaded me to come.'

'Good move?'

'Oh, yes, for all sorts of reasons. Nice town, and the hospital's great, much nicer to work in than my previous one, and—well, further from someone I needed space from.'

Now why had she brought that up? Idiot! She could see the question forming in his eyes, but she was saved from having to explain by their arrival at the restaurant, and by the time they were seated and the waiter had given them menus and water and a basket of warm, squashy bread, they'd moved on.

Thankfully.

'So why obstetrics?' he asked her, reaching for the bread.

'I love it. Less keen on the gynae, except some of the surgery's quite interesting and technically challenging, but mostly it's the babies. Making a difference, saving such vulnerable little lives— I'm a sucker for it. The friend I told you about's a midwife, and I guess she influenced me a bit. You?'

He shrugged. 'All sorts of reasons, really. My

father's a vet and my brother and I used to go out with him on calls sometimes when we were kids. We helped with the lambing and the calving, and sometimes there'd be a foal, and I just loved it. And of course all the cats and dogs had litters, and we always watched them giving birth, and my mother's a midwife, so when I went into medicine it just seemed the obvious choice. My brother's an obstetrician, too, but he's a bit more focussed on his career than me.' He gave a wry smile. 'It's been a bit difficult recently. Life sort of threw a spanner in the works.'

'That's divorce for you,' she said without thinking, and could have bitten her tongue off, but he just shrugged again and smiled sadly.

'Yes, it is. Are you divorced?'

'Me? No! Single and proud of it,' she lied. Well, not about the single part, because she was, profoundly, since Mike had walked away, but she wasn't proud of it. She was more—well, lonely, really, she admitted, but she'd rather be single than in the situation she'd been in. And for all the difference it would have made, in many ways she felt divorced. Would have been, if Mike had ever got round to asking her to marry him instead of just stringing her along for years. She scraped up a chirpy grin. 'Mad spinster lady, that's what I am. Didn't you notice the cat?'

'I thought you had to have more than one to be a mad spinster?' he said softly, his eyes searching even though there was a smile teasing his lips, and she felt her heart turn over.

No! No no no no no!

'Oh, well, I've only got the one, so that's all right, then, I'm not a spinster, just mad,' she said lightly, and turned her attention to the menu. Fast.

Ben watched her. She was distracted, not concentrating. The menu was the right way up, but it could have been in Russian or Japanese for all the difference it would have made, he was sure. She was flustered—by him?

Interesting—except that she was a colleague, and his neighbour, and he'd just got out of one horribly messy relationship and he was in no hurry to get into another.

Even if she was the most attractive, interesting and stimulating person he'd been near in what felt like decades.

He shut his menu with a snap, and her body gave a tiny little jerk, as if the sound had startled her. 'I'm having the pan-fried sea bass,' he said briskly. 'What about you?'

'Um…' She stared at the menu, blinked and nodded. 'Sounds nice,' she said, and he would have laid odds she hadn't even seen the print, never mind made sense of it.

'Wine?'

Stupid. Utterly stupid, on a week night, with work the next day.

'I could have a glass, I suppose,' she said thoughtfully.

'Sauvignon blanc?'

She nodded, and the light from the candle caught her hair and it shimmered like rich, dark silk. He wanted to reach over and catch a strand between thumb and forefinger, wind it round his fingertip and reel her in, tugging her gently towards him until those soft, full lips were in range, and then—

'Are you ready to order, sir?'

He straightened up, sucking in a slow, silent breath and raising an eyebrow at Daisy. 'Have you decided?'

'Oh—um—the sea bass, like you?' she said, saving him from the embarrassment of admitting he'd forgotten everything except the shimmer of her hair and the soft sheen of her lips.

'Sounds good,' he said, and added the wine to the list. A couple of glasses wouldn't make any difference…

'That was really nice. Thank you, Ben,' she said, hesitating by her front gate.

They'd walked back side by side, fingers brushing from time to time, shoulders nudging gently. Not holding hands, but not far off it, and she wondered, just idly—well, no, not idly at all, really—if he was going to kiss her goodnight.

Madness! Too much wine. She shouldn't have had the second glass.

'My pleasure. I'd offer you coffee, but the cafetière was in the box that jingled,' he told her ruefully, and she smiled.

'I've got coffee,' she told him before she could stop her mouth, and their eyes locked and he lifted his shoulders in an almost imperceptible shrug.

'Coffee would be nice. Thank you.'

She unlocked her door, and he followed her in, all the way through to the kitchen. It was open to the dining area, and she directed him to the table to get herself a little space.

'Make yourself comfortable,' she said, and switched the kettle on, glancing at the clock as she did so. Heavens, they'd been out for well over two hours. It was after eleven o'clock, and she had to be on the ward tomorrow at eight. Silly. She shouldn't have invited him in. Too late, and way too dangerous.

She frowned into the freezer, searching for the coffee, and then gave up and opened a new packet. She had no idea how long the other one had been open and her mind didn't seem to want to work it out.

'Black or white, and hot or cold milk?' she asked, sloshing hot water into the cafetière to warm it.

'Black, one sugar,' he said.

Of course. That was how he'd had it in the bistro, although he'd had a latte in the hospital that morning. Heavens. Was it only that morning? It seemed aeons ago!

Her thoughts miles away, she picked up the tray and found herself heading automatically to the sitting room at the front of the house. She'd meant to put it down on the dining table, but before she could change tack he'd stood up and was following. Damn! It would be too cosy in there, much too intimate, and the wine was fogging her brain.

The wine, and the company…

'Oh, this room's lovely, Daisy,' he said warmly as she put the coffee down, and she felt herself glow with his praise.

'Thanks. Do you want some music on?'

'Shall I?' He was crouching down in front of her iPod dock without waiting for an answer, scrolling through her music collection, making himself at home. He put on something soft and romantic, and she could hardly tell him she didn't like it, as it was her music. And she'd sat down already, so it was impossible to choose the other sofa when he sat at the other end of hers, a perfectly respectable distance from her and yet just close enough that her nose could pick up the scent of that citrusy cologne he'd been wearing this morning.

It had been teasing her nostrils all evening, and she could have leant against him and breathed him in.

Except that it wouldn't make any sense at all,

and if she knew what was good for her she'd drink her coffee and send him on his way.

Except it didn't quite work like that.

They talked and laughed until long after the coffee was finished, and then finally he sighed and got to his feet.

'I ought to go.'

'Yes, you should,' she said, and stood up, but she'd kicked off her shoes and she tripped on one and he caught her, his hands strong and steady on her arms.

'OK?' he murmured, and she lifted her head and met his eyes and everything seemed to stop dead.

Her heart, her lungs, the clock—everything froze in that moment, and then as if someone had thrown a switch and set him free, he bent his head, so slowly that she had all the time in the world to move away, and touched his lips to hers.

She sighed his name, her heart kicking back into life like a wild thing, and then his arms were sliding round her and he was kissing her properly.

Improperly?

He tasted of coffee and after dinner mints, his

tongue bold and persuasive, coaxing her, leading her, then retreating, making her follow.

She was putty in his hands, all her senses short-circuited by the gentle, rhythmic stroke of his tongue, the soft brush of his lips, the warm whisper of his breath over her face as he sipped and touched and lingered.

If he'd led her upstairs, she would have followed, but he didn't. Instead he lifted his head and rested his chin on her hair and cradled her gently against his chest.

'I really ought to go,' he said again, but his voice was gruff this time, the soft Yorkshire burr teasing her senses, and his arms stayed wrapped around her.

She lay there another moment listening to the steady, insistent thud of his heart against her ear, and then reluctantly she dropped her arms from round his waist and stepped back.

'Yes, you should. Thank you for taking me out. You really didn't need to, but it was lovely. I really enjoyed it.'

'So did I. I'd like to do it again, but I'm not sure if that's wise. We work together, we live next door. It could get messy.'

She nodded, struggling against an inexplicable urge to cry. 'Yeah. Lousy idea.' And he was divorced. She didn't do that. Didn't do anything. Not any more.

He took a step towards the door, then turned back, his eyes lingering on her face. 'Thank you for everything today. You've been amazing.'

She tried to smile. 'Any time.'

He lifted a hand and his knuckles grazed her cheek tenderly. 'Goodnight, Daisy. Sleep well. I'll see you tomorrow.'

She nodded. She couldn't speak, because for some ridiculous reason she was on the verge of tears, and as if he knew that, he gave a sad, fleeting little smile and let himself out.

CHAPTER THREE

WORKWISE, Tuesday was a day like any other.

On a personal level, Daisy thought she was going to go out of her mind. She'd hardly slept, and by the time she arrived on the ward, she'd convinced herself that working with Ben was going to be impossible.

In fact, it was easy.

He greeted her with a smile, and if it hadn't been for the lingering heat in his eyes, she wouldn't have known anything had happened between them. It was just business as usual.

No cosy coffees today, just the normal routine of a busy surgical list, including an elective Caesarean on a woman with an old spinal injury who had to have a general anaesthetic rather than an epidural. It was a good chance for him to see what she could do, and he could talk her through it without worrying the patient or her partner.

Although, in fact, he hardly said anything, just

nodded reassurance and made the odd suggestion, and then stripped off his gloves and walked out. 'You're doing fine. You close, I'm going to get a coffee. Bit of a late night.'

Evil man. Thank God for a mask she could hide her smile behind, and the scrub nurse and anaesthetist deep in conversation about another colleague.

She finished, stripped off her gloves and went out to the staffroom, to find him pouring another coffee and holding it out to her as she approached.

'Nice,' he said. 'Good hands. You remind me of my father.'

'Is that a good thing?' she asked, not sure she was flattered.

'It is if you're a good vet.'

'Like James Herriot? All stone barns and stroppy farmers?'

He chuckled. 'Things have moved on since the forties. You've got the makings of an excellent surgeon, though.'

'Just don't get me delivering calves.'

The silly banter was just what she needed to take her mind off what had happened last night—

or not happened. Except of course the tension between them was still there, the incredible sexual chemistry striking sparks off her every time she was within twenty feet of him. And of all the people for it to happen with—

'Hey, it's OK,' he murmured softly, as if he realised, and then the anaesthetist stuck his head round the door and gave them the thumbs up.

'She's round, she's fine. Ready for the next?'

He got to his feet and went to scrub, and when she'd drained her coffee she joined him and the awkward, sensitive moment was gone.

For now.

Ben closed the front door behind him, rolled his neck and cradled it in his palm, massaging the tight muscles.

He'd been operating most of the day, and on top of lugging boxes all weekend, it was getting to him. Not forgetting lying awake thinking about Daisy all night.

He groaned and shut his eyes. He really, really didn't need to think about that. It had been difficult enough having to work alongside her all day without coming home and fantasising about her all evening as well.

He put the kettle on, rang the plumber back about the electrician and the plasterer, and made himself a cup of tea. He'd just dropped into a chair in his sitting room to drink it when his mobile rang.

'So how's the new house?'

He gave a slightly strangled laugh and looked around at the hideous 1970s wallpaper and the dangling paper on the ceiling. When he closed his eyes, all he could see was the trashed kitchen. 'Let's just say it's got potential.'

'Oops.'

'Yeah. The bath waste wasn't properly connected.'

'And?'

'I don't have a kitchen ceiling now.'

'OK…' His brother was stifling a laugh, he could tell, and he could feel his own lips twitch.

'You ought to come up and see it.'

Matt didn't bother to stifle the laugh then. 'You have to be kidding. You'll have me stripping wallpaper and pulling out kitchen units before

I've taken my coat off,' he said drily, and then added, 'So, how's the job? Any good?'

'Yes, very good. The SpR's a bit of an old woman, but the registrar's excellent. Good team.'

'And your neighbours? Met them yet?'

'Ah—yes. Actually, the registrar's my neighbour. She's in the other half.'

'Is *she*, now?'

Ben closed his eyes and leant back. 'Yes, *she* is. And she was very helpful about the leak. I took her out for dinner to say thank you,' he added rashly, and he heard Matt's curiosity crank up a notch.

'And?'

'And nothing.'

Matt was laughing. 'Oh, come on, bro, I know you better than that. I thought you were sounding pretty chipper. So let's have it. What's her name?'

'Daisy.'

'*Daisy*! What kind of a name is that?'

'Don't mock, you're only jealous.'

'Ooh, defensive—that's interesting! So what's she like?'

'Average height, curvy, long dark hair, green eyes, sexy mouth—'

'Really? How sexy?'

Damn. He sighed and shut his eyes. 'Didn't mean to say that.'

He heard a low chuckle. 'I'll bet. How sexy?'

He gave up. 'She kisses like a goddess,' he admitted, and there was a second of startled silence on the other end.

Then, '*When* did you meet her?'

'Yesterday.'

'And you know how she *kisses*? *Already*? Sheesh, that's fast work! And she's a *colleague*? You're normally much more circumspect. She must have really lit a fire under you.'

Oh, yes. For all the good it'd do. 'It's not going anywhere. You know I'm not in the market for a relationship, Matt, any more than you are.'

'So who's talking about a relationship?' Matt asked with his usual bluntness, and he sighed again.

'She's a nice girl, not someone you take to bed for the hell of it.'

'I thought you grew out of that years ago.'

'Yeah, well, I nearly forgot.'

Matt blew out his breath. 'It must have been

some kiss.' He sounded incredulous, and Ben ran a hand round the back of his neck and sighed.

'Yeah. Big mistake, kissing her. We—uh—we got a bit swept along on the moment, and we shouldn't have done. I should have had more sense, and I know it's crazy, and I keep telling myself it can't go anywhere, but—hell, I was so tempted to stay, Matt. I was that close...'

He heard her front door shut, and shook his head to clear it. 'Look, I've got to go, she's home now and these walls aren't exactly soundproof. I think I'm going round there to talk to her—tell her why it can't ever go anywhere before she gets ideas.'

'Are you sure it can't?' Matt prompted, his voice soft. 'Maybe it's time to move on—find some time for yourself.'

And because he wanted it to be otherwise, because he was blown away by Daisy and wanted to be able to follow through but knew he couldn't—or wouldn't—Ben bit back.

'I don't see you moving on with your life,' he said, and he heard Matt suck in his breath again.

'Back off,' he warned softly.

'Sorry, ignore me. Well, no, don't ignore me.

Come up here and stay for a few days. It would be really good to see you and I promise I won't make you strip wallpaper.'

'I don't believe a word of it, but I might come anyway, just to get a look at this Daisy. Good luck with her. I'll look forward to meeting her one day.'

The line went dead, and he stood up and went out to the kitchen with his mug. He'd give Daisy a few minutes to change and feed the cat, and then he'd go round there.

And stop this thing in its tracks.

She wanted a bath. She'd wanted a bath since Sunday night, and nothing that had happened in the meantime had changed that.

She stared at it, sitting there taunting her with its promise of gentle, lapping water and utter relaxation. She still hadn't unpacked from the weekend, there was washing waiting to go in the machine, and—

'Oh, damn it,' she said, and turned on the taps, poured in a generous dollop of bubble bath, and while the delectably indulgent Victorian claw-foot bath filled with water, she put on some music, turned down the lights and lit a scented candle, then dropped her clothes into the laundry basket, stepped into the bath and slid under the bubbles.

'Oh, yes,' she groaned. Bliss.

Except she was twitchy. She could hear Ben moving around next door, unpacking probably. He was going to come round, she just knew it, and catching her in the bath really wouldn't help. She'd have to run down to the front door looking like a drowned rat, and what little was left of her pride would go straight out of the window.

She rinsed her hair in clean water, dragged herself reluctantly out of the bath, dried and picked up her dressing gown. It still had a tea stain all the way down the front, and there was no way she could wear it again until it had been washed. She really *had* to do her laundry.

She contemplated her baggy old sweats, and then put on jeans and last night's top, because she just had a feeling he'd be round. No reason. He hadn't said he would, but better to be prepared. And she resisted the urge to change the top for one he hadn't seen.

She'd dry her hair, and put on a touch of makeup—just a flick of mascara and some concealer under her eyes to hide the bags, because two nights without sleep showed on her fair skin—and then she'd unpack and tidy her room.

Not that she needed to worry about Ben seeing it, anyway, she thought with irony as she dabbed on the concealer. He'd been the one to walk away, while she'd been teetering on the brink.

And in any case, what on earth was she *thinking*? She didn't *want* him in her bedroom! There was no way she was getting involved with another divorced man, because she was still dealing with the devastating emotional fallout from the last one. And he was her boss! *And* her neighbour!

'Huge great big fat no, Daisy,' she said firmly, and picked up her mascara.

She heard him run downstairs, then the sound of his door closing. A moment later, there was a knock on her own door, and even though she'd tried to convince herself it was the last thing she wanted, her heart raced with anticipation and her hands started to shake.

She put the mascara down before she could poke her eye out, went downstairs and opened the door.

He had flowers. A huge bunch of pure white longiflorum lilies, the scent astonishing, and he held them out to her.

'Are you trying to soften me up or is this a peace offering for trying to take advantage of my innocence?' she asked, taking them from him warily, and he felt his mouth kick up in a wry smile. If he'd wanted to take advantage of her innocence, he wouldn't have had to try very hard, she'd been with him every step of the way...

'Neither. I thought they'd mask the smell of damp plaster clinging to me.'

She gave a disbelieving little laugh and walked off, and he followed her through the door she'd left open—presumably for him—to the kitchen. She was putting the flowers in a tall vase and fiddling with them, pulling off leaves, trying to arrange the stubborn stems, and he could tell she was nervous.

Why? In case he tried anything again? No way. She was safe on that front, at least.

'Have you eaten?' he asked, and she felt her brow crease in a little frown.

'No. Not yet. I was going to have that ready

meal.' *Don't ask me out again, Ben, please, don't ask me out.*

'Can I change your mind? I thought maybe we could find a pub somewhere, grab something to eat and have a chat.'

Her stomach fluttered, and she squashed the quiver of anticipation ruthlessly. 'I don't really want to go out. I could do with an early night, to be honest,' she lied, and jammed another lily stem into the vase.

He watched her thoughtfully. 'Is that, "Ben, sling your hook," or "I don't want to go out but we could have a takeaway"?' he asked, trying to read her body language.

She gave up on arranging the flowers and dumped the vase in the middle of the dining table. 'Neither. Ben, why are you here?' she asked a little desperately.

He propped himself up against the table next to her, hands thrust into his trouser pockets, and sighed quietly.

'I think we need to talk about what happened last night.'

'Nothing happened last night.'

His laugh was low and mocking. 'Get real,

Daisy. We were *that* close.' He held up his hand, his thumb and forefinger almost touching, and she felt heat pooling in her at the memory.

She made herself meet his eyes, and then regretted it, because they were glittering with an intensity that should have terrified her.

It *did* terrify her.

She looked away. 'Well, spit it out, then, because you've obviously got something to get off your chest,' she said briskly, and she felt the huff of his quiet laugh against her cheek.

'It's—complicated.'

She gave a derisive snort and straightened one of the lily stems. 'The last man to say that told me he was going back to his wife and family,' she said drily, and he found himself wondering about the bastard who'd hurt her.

'I'm not going to say that, exactly.'

She felt relief try and break free, but sensed it was a little early and squashed it. And that 'exactly' was hanging in the air like an unexploded bomb. 'So what *are* you saying, *exactly*?' she prompted. 'That you're my boss and it's a bad idea? You're divorced? We're neighbours? I've already worked all that out, and I absolutely agree.'

'I have a daughter,' he said, dropping the bombshell of all bombshells without preamble. 'She's nearly three, and she's called Florence. That's why I'm here, why I'm in Yoxburgh. My ex moved back to be near her family and friends, and I've followed.'

Here we go again, she thought, and her heart sank. 'Because you want to get back with her and she won't play ball?'

'No way. To be near Florence, so I can take an active role in her day-to-day life. There's no way we're getting back together—'

'I've heard that before, too,' she said bluntly, still curiously reeling with disappointment, but that was silly. He'd said nothing, done nothing. No lies, no promises. He hadn't spun her any kind of line at all, unlike Mike. He'd just been himself, easy, charming, relaxed, funny, and she'd—what? Fallen for him? Even though she'd known he was trouble?

'But *I* mean it. We won't be getting back together. Our marriage was a disaster and I have no intention of revisiting it. The only reason I've moved up here is for Florence, and she has to come first before anything.'

'Well, good. It's refreshing to hear a father say that,' she said with feeling, 'but I can't see what it's got to do with us.'

'It's why there won't be an "us", in any meaningful way,' he said gently. 'I owe it to Florence to make her life as uncomplicated and normal as it can be for a little girl with two parents who can't live with each other, and amongst other things, that means no "aunties" drifting in and out of her life, so if you're harbouring any illusions about this going any further, then I'm sorry, Daisy, I'm not in the market for it.'

Harbouring any illusions? The only illusion she'd harboured was the notion that he might be free and unencumbered. Not *a father*! How could she have been so naïve that it hadn't even occurred to her?

And now she knew he had a daughter, there was no way she'd touch him with a bargepole! She'd been here before, and two little girls had been desperately hurt when he'd decided he loved his wife after all and she was going to forgive him for his endless indiscretions and have him back.

'Don't flatter yourself, I'm not harbouring anything,' she told him straight. 'And the last thing I need in my life is another relationship with a man with a ton of emotional baggage, so relax, Ben. You're safe. I'm not even slightly interested.'

He gave a soft laugh. 'Well, that's me told,' he said, and wondered why on earth her emphatic rejection should matter quite so much.

'You don't need to be too injured. Without the baggage I could have been very interested,' she added rashly. 'I just don't have a death wish, so I don't do family men. One of my rules. Out of curiosity,' she went on, 'why didn't you tell me about your daughter yesterday?'

He frowned. 'I'm sorry, I didn't realise it would be such a big deal to you,' he said. 'I wasn't deliberately keeping her a secret, although I don't talk about her or any other aspect of my private life to people I don't know, but by the time we'd reached a point when I might well have told you, I wasn't exactly thinking clearly, and neither were you, if you remember.'

Oh, didn't she just—but he'd walked away, in the nick of time.

'Nothing happened, Ben,' she reminded him

firmly, 'and I don't expect anything to. As I said, I'm not interested.'

His shoulders dropped, and he nodded slowly. 'Good. I think.'

'You think?' she asked warily.

He shrugged, his mouth twisting into a fleeting, rueful smile. He ought to leave it alone, really, to drop the subject and move on, but honesty compelled him to explain.

'I'm torn, Daisy,' he told her. 'And it sounds like you could be, too. It's a lousy idea, as I said last night, but I'm not made of stone, and I really like you. And in an ideal world—well, it might all be very different. It would be nice to see you outside work, get to know you, spend time with you, but I don't think it would be fair on you. You aren't the kind of girl for a casual fling, and I can't offer you anything more serious at this point in my life. I don't want you getting hurt—I don't want either of us getting hurt, come to that, and I won't have Florence hurt under any circumstances, but there's no future in it for us, and I'm still your colleague—'

'Well, if we're going to be brutally honest

you're my boss,' she pointed out frankly, and he felt his mouth twitch again.

'I'm still your *colleague*,' he repeated, 'we have to work together, and I can't afford to jeopardise that. I have to make a success of this job, for my sake and for Florence's, and there's no way I can give you any kind of happy ever after. My marriage really screwed me up. I put everything I had into it, even though I knew it wasn't perfect, but it wasn't enough, and it nearly tore me apart. I'm never going there again.'

Oh, Ben, she thought. She'd been there, felt the same way when Mike had walked out and taken his daughters with him. She'd done everything she could, and it just hadn't been enough.

'I'm sorry,' she said softly. 'I know how that feels, I really do.'

He nodded, and reached out a hand, squeezing her shoulder gently. His touch warmed her, and she wanted to lean into him, to lay her head against his chest and stay there.

Instead she moved away, going to the kettle to put it on.

'So that's both of us nursing a broken heart.'

'Nursing a whole heap of disillusion and disappointment,' he corrected quietly, but making a very large and clear note to himself that her heart was broken. 'And the last thing I need is to get involved with someone with the same history.'

Especially after Jane—Jane, who'd been on the rebound when he'd met her. Never again.

'You're right. It would be crazy. Ben, I'm hungry, I need to eat,' she said, wondering if it was low blood sugar making her feel a little light-headed, or the conversation. 'I'm going to heat up this ready meal.'

'Or we could share a takeaway,' he said, changing tack, not quite ready to end this time with her, needing to get their relationship as friends and colleagues and neighbours firmly on track and lay the ghost of that kiss. 'I have an ulterior motive. I want to ask your advice about my house.'

She stared at him, bit her lip, shrugged. 'I don't know that I can be much use, I know very little about your house. Apart from the other day, I've only been in it a few times, and I've never been upstairs except to fetch something for Mrs Leggatt once.'

'But you know this house, and I love what I've

seen of it, which let's face it is pretty much all of it. Come and have a look. I'll order a takeaway, and while it's coming, you can cast your eye over it and tell me what you'd do,' he coaxed. 'Unless you'd rather not?'

She laughed softly. 'I'd love to see round it,' she said honestly, and tipped her head on one side. 'Can we have Chinese?'

'Sure. Got a menu?'

'Of course I have. I've got a stack of them. They get put through the door all the time. We're quite civilised round here.'

'Great. And we can wash it down with the bubbly you gave me yesterday. It seems only fair to share it.'

'I don't think that would be a good idea,' she said carefully.

'Maybe not,' he conceded with a rueful smile, and held his hand out. 'Let's have the menu, then. I'm ravenous.'

He saw Florence the following evening.

He couldn't bring her home for the night, which was the eventual plan for Wednesdays, because it was in chaos following the ceiling collapse and would be for some time, so he spent the evening with her at Jane's.

Difficult, because although they'd parted on reasonable terms, it was her house, and technically speaking her night off.

'Do you mind if I go out?' she asked, and he agreed readily. It would be easier without her, would give him a more relaxed and focussed time with Florence, and would mean less of a change when she did eventually come to him.

So he stayed there with Florence, and he cooked her supper and bathed her, and then tucked her up into bed and lay beside her with her snuggled into the crook of his arm while he read her a bedtime story.

'Again,' she said when he'd finished.

He read it again. It was easier than arguing, and easier than reading her another book—because that could lead to another, and another, and another—and he'd been suckered before. Not yet three, and she was a clever little minx.

He adored her.

'Again,' she said, but sleepily this time, her thumb in her mouth. She'd started nursery school full time because Jane wanted to go back to work, and she was loving it, but she was tired by the end of the day and he guessed that if Jane had been reading the story, she would have fallen asleep sooner.

Bedtime with Daddy was a novelty, though, her time with him limited, and she was often clingy.

So he read it again, and then eased his arm incredibly carefully out from under her head, lowering it to the pillow and kissing her softly on her rosy little cheek as she slept.

'Goodnight, my precious,' he murmured, smoothing the hair back from her face as his eyes filled. 'Sleep tight.'

He kissed her again, and left the room, her door ajar and a nightlight on in case she woke, and then he went downstairs and sat on the sofa they'd had in London and watched his old television until Jane came home at ten.

'Everything all right?' she asked brightly, and there was something in her tone of voice that made him search her face as he got to his feet.

'Fine. She's asleep. We read *Goldilocks and the Three Bears* three times.'

'Oh, Ben, you have to learn to say no.'

'No, I don't. I have to make her happy and bond

with her, so she feels secure with me. We spent too much time apart before I moved up here, and I've got ground to make up. Anyway, reading to her isn't exactly a hardship.'

She nodded, then as he was leaving she said carefully, 'So, are you planning on sleeping here this weekend?'

'Yes, if that's all right, otherwise I won't be here when she wakes up, so she'll disturb you and that's not fair.' And he'd miss that lovely morning snuggle. 'I can't have her at the house for ages, but if it's a problem I can maybe sort something out.'

'No, it's not a problem. I was just wondering—if you're going to be staying over anyway, do you mind if I'm not here on Saturday night? Well, from Saturday morning to Sunday evening, really.'

There was definitely something different about her. She looked—what? Happier? He shrugged. Why should he mind? It was easier than feeling guilty about ruining her life, and he resisted the urge to ask where she was going. It was none of his business, unless it affected Florence—and it didn't. 'That's fine. Do whatever. I might bring some washing over to do, if it's OK?'

'Of course it is—you pay the bills, Ben. And I might have got a job lined up, by the way, which should make things easier. It's not certain yet, but—who knows?'

She smiled, and he realised she did look happy—maybe because of the job, or maybe not. And he also realised he'd never really seen her look this happy before.

What a sad indictment of their marriage. No wonder it had failed so spectacularly.

'Well, I hope it works out for you,' he said, fishing for his keys in his pocket. 'Right, I'm off, I'll see you on Friday.'

He drove home, his heart aching at leaving his little daughter behind. He hated not being part of her everyday routine—not sharing her bathtime and bedtime, her breakfast, taking her to nursery, not being there to cuddle her when she woke in the night.

Just not being there for her.

Still, he'd have the weekend alone with her, or most of it, and they'd be able to stay at the house and just chill out together. Maybe he'd buy her a swing and put it up in the garden—or maybe he'd do that at his own house in a few weeks' time, once it was a bit more sorted. Then she'd have a proper home with him here, too, with toys and things, and maybe she'd be a bit more settled.

He pulled up outside, cut the engine and stared longingly at Daisy's house.

The lights were on, and he was so tempted. He hesitated by his front door, debated stepping over the silly little fence and going to see her, and crushed the urge. He couldn't keep going round there. It was self-indulgent and intrusive, not to mention downright dangerous. He was drawn to her like a moth to a flame, and the *last* thing he needed was another woman on the rebound.

And he needed to find something more mentally involving to do at work than have Daisy assist him in Theatre. It gave him too much time to think about her while he operated on autopilot.

He'd let her lead tomorrow. He'd have to teach her, then, and there were some interesting cases on his gynae list.

And maybe it would keep his mind a little more firmly on the job and off his obsessive preoccupation with his registrar...

CHAPTER FOUR

IT WAS odd not seeing him after work on Wednesday. Wednesdays were his night for Florence, he said, and he'd be back late.

She didn't miss him. Of course she didn't! She'd only just met him, so how could the house feel empty if he wasn't there? She was just bored, and catching up with the washing—never her favourite task but she needed her dressing gown back and she was running out of underwear. And she'd finally eaten the ready meal, the solitary little portion underlining her pathetic single status.

Not that her status was any different to this time last week, but it somehow *felt* different. It was the kiss that had done it, she thought. The kiss, and talking to him, sharing smiles and the odd joke at work. Going round to his house last night and seeing the full extent of what he'd taken on.

Making friends slowly, day by day.

Actually, not that slowly, and working with him was a privilege and a joy. It was living next to him and wanting the man and not the doctor that was so hard, because if the doctor was wonderful, the man was downright off the scale.

She heard him come in at ten, and she wondered if he'd knock on her door. Bring round a bottle of wine, or ask her to go there for coffee. And then maybe he'd kiss her goodnight...

She slammed the washing machine door shut, put the iron away and shoved the basket into the corner. She'd deal with the sheets and towels tomorrow, she decided, and went to bed, irritated that he had the power to affect her both with his presence and his absence. Ridiculous!

Anyway, she needed an early night, and the next day she was glad she'd had one. Ben had a busy gynae list and asked her to assist—which meant in practice he got her to lead on several of the ops, so that she did most of the surgery and he held instruments and handled the suction and told her what to do.

It was his job to mentor her after all, and she appreciated it, but he took it very seriously and stretched her to the limit, testing her ability all through the day so that she was exhausted by the time the last patient was in Recovery.

Exhausted and proud of herself, she thought as she showered. She'd done far more than she ever had before, and she'd been able to do it because he had confidence in her.

Unlike Evan, who still double-checked her work and seemed unable to delegate.

She raised it with Ben as they sat in her conservatory drinking tea after she'd got home, and he shrugged. 'That's his problem,' he said. 'I don't have any problem delegating to you. I think he lacks confidence in himself, to be honest, and I don't think he's ready to be a consultant. What do you think of this one?'

He'd brought round a bunch of kitchen brochures the plumber had dropped in, and they were flicking through them while they waited for the takeaway to be delivered. Thai, this time, for a change. His choice. His bill again, he said, as he was commandeering her time to get her advice on his kitchen refit.

It was a safe topic, well clear of the minefield of his personal life—and hers, come to that. Not that she had one, unless you counted the cat.

Safer than talking about her feelings, anyway, because she certainly had *them* and they were getting more complex with every passing day.

The food arrived, and it was getting cooler in the conservatory so they ate in the dining room, with soft music in the background and the lights on low.

A mistake, she realised, because it made it very intimate, and suddenly it began to feel like a date, all over again.

He'd brought the bubbly with him as a bribe for her input into his kitchen, and whether it was that, or the intimate atmosphere, or just that the chemistry between them was so all-consuming that it wiped out everything in its path, she didn't know.

All she knew was that everything he said made her laugh, and when he smiled his eyes lit up and his whole face joined in. And he was just so *nice*, so ordinary and yet extraordinary, unlike all the other men she'd ever met before.

They drained the bottle between them—foolish, she thought, on a work night, but after the first sip she was past caring—and she made some coffee and they took it through to the sitting room.

Was it that? Returning to the scene of the crime? Or was it the bubbly? She didn't know, but when at last he looked at his watch and got to his feet, she followed him to the door and he turned and took her in his arms and hugged her briefly.

'Thank you, Daisy. You did amazingly well today. And you've been really helpful over all this kitchen planning nonsense. I couldn't have done it without you, I wouldn't have thought of half those points.'

'You're welcome. I have just done it, so I know what the pitfalls are. And thank *you*, anyway. You bought the dinner—again. And you shared the bubbly.'

His mouth twitched into a smile. 'But I stole your brains. Fair exchange.'

He had. Stolen her brains. All of them. If he hadn't, she wouldn't have gone up on tiptoe and kissed him, touching her lips lightly to the corner of that smiling mouth, the slight rasp of stubble on his lean, male cheek making them tingle. She wouldn't have turned her head so that their lips collided.

And when he groaned and slid his arms around her, she wouldn't have curled hers around his neck and threaded her fingers through his soft, silky hair and given him her mouth.

He took it with a low moan, sipping and tasting and coaxing, and by the time he lifted his head she was beyond coherent thought.

'Daisy, I have to go,' he said, his voice a little roughened.

No! Stay. Please stay. Make love to me.

Their eyes locked, and he let out a shaky sigh. 'Don't,' he whispered soundlessly.

'Don't what?' she croaked, wondering for a hideous second if she could have said it out loud.

'Don't look at me like that.'

Her heart stuttered. 'Like what?' she whispered.

'Like *that*,' he said fervently, cradling her cheek in his palm, his thumb tracing her cheekbone. 'As if—oh, hell, this is such a lousy idea,' he muttered as his mouth found hers again, and she went up on tiptoe and opened her mouth to him and whimpered as he took it in a kiss so hungry, so urgent, so fiercely needy that it rocked her world.

'*Daisy...!*'

The groan tore through him, echoing in her body, ricocheting around inside it and unsettling all her fragile resolve.

She wanted him. It was sheer lunacy, but he was perfect, everything she'd ever wanted in a man, and she needed him *so much...*

'Ben...'

He lifted his head and searched her eyes, his own almost black with this incredible need that seemed to have sprung up out of nowhere and caught them both in its grip.

She moved away a fraction, to give him a chance, and waited, her hand held out to him. For a breathless, endless age he stood there, those dark eyes trapping hers, and then, just when she thought he was going, he lifted his hand, threaded his fingers through hers and locked them tight.

She led him upstairs to her bedroom on legs that could hardly support her weight.

Her case was still lying on the floor, there was a pile of clean underwear on the top of the chest of drawers and her work clothes were scattered all over the carpet where she'd dropped them, but they picked their way through the chaos to the bed, and then he turned her into his arms and brushed his lips lightly over hers.

His eyes were serious. 'Are you sure you want to do this?'

Sure? Not really. Want? Absolutely. It was the craziest thing she'd done in years, but if she couldn't hold him, touch him, feel him—

She nodded, and he slid his wallet out of his pocket and pulled a little foil packet out and put it on the side. Her lids fluttered closed. He wasn't going. He was going to stay, going to make love to her.

And how. His fingers gathered up the hem of her top and drew it carefully over her head, his breath catching as he looked down at her, and she was glad she'd washed her favourite bra.

The clip gave to the touch of his hand, and then her breasts were spilling into his hands, and with a deep groan he ducked his head and grazed his lips over the soft, sweet flesh he'd exposed.

He didn't know what he was doing here. He was past caring, past thinking rationally. He just knew he needed Daisy as he'd never needed any woman, and if he didn't have her in the next few minutes, he was going to explode.

And he had a feeling it was mutual.

Her eyes were wild, her soft, sweet lips parted, her head tipped back as he suckled deeply on first one taut, pebbled nipple and then the other.

'Ben…!'

'I'm right here, Daisy,' he grated, his breath heaving, his heart trying to escape from his chest, and her hands were on him, pulling his shirt out and flattening her palms against his ribcage, gasping as he tugged down the zip of her jeans and eased them over the ripe, sweet swell of her hips so he could cup her bottom and drag her up against him.

Oh, lord, she was going to go up in flames! His skin was hot, taut over the muscles beneath. She wanted more, wanted to feel the rest of him, wanted to touch him, hold him, look at him, but her fingers were struggling with his belt, and she was whimpering with frustration. If she couldn't get his belt undone—

He swatted her hands aside gently and ripped the shirt off, dealt with the belt and the stud and the zip and shucked the lot in one hasty and desperate movement, and her legs buckled.

She gasped as he pulled her back into his arms and their bodies came firmly into contact from top to toe. Well, knee. Her jeans were still there, but not for much longer, apparently. He lifted her as if she weighed nothing, dropped her into the middle of the bed, stripped off her jeans and came down beside her, the condom in his hands.

'Let me,' she said, taking it from him with her trembling, uncoordinated fingers. The first intimate touch of her hands made him suck in his breath in a shuddering groan, and then he was rolling her under him and sinking into her, filling her, and her scream cut through the air.

He shifted up a gear, drove into her and felt her rising to meet him, her body straining against his.

'Ben, please! I need…'

'I'm here,' he growled. 'I'm right with you, Daisy. Come with me—please, come with me.'

He felt her body tighten, heard her breath catch as she bucked against him, and then he was lost in a climax so devastating that he thought he might have died.

As the last shudders faded from their taut, sweat-slicked bodies, he rolled them to their sides, gathered her into his arms and closed his eyes.

He felt in shock. Never before. Not like that. He heard her breathing slow, and then another shudder, a tiny one, almost a sob, ran through her and he cradled her gently against his heart and held her while the last of the emotions roiling through them faded to a more manageable level.

Then, and only then, did he open his eyes and move his head so he could see her face.

It was streaked with tears, her eyes soft and luminous, her mouth swollen and rosy from his kisses, and he brushed his knuckles lightly over her cheek.

'Are you OK?' he murmured.

'I think so. Not sure. If you let me have my brain back, maybe I can work it out?'

It was so ridiculous he started to laugh, and once he started, he couldn't stop. Neither could she, and they lay there all but sobbing with laughter as the last dregs of emotion ebbed away. Then she lifted her hand and touched his face, her fingertips brushing lightly over the tiny cut above his eyebrow.

'That was amazing, Ben,' she said softly, and her eyes were so nakedly revealing he felt guilt tear through him, because he shouldn't have done it, shouldn't have touched her, held her, taken that sweet, precious gift she'd offered.

They were destined for disaster. What the hell had he been thinking about?

He closed his eyes and rolled away from her. 'I need to deal with this,' he said, and headed for the bathroom, leaving her lying there feeling a little foolish and vulnerable in the aftermath of so much raw emotion. She scooted under the quilt and sat up, hugging her knees, waiting for him to come back from the bathroom and tell her it had all been a mistake.

As if she didn't know that!

Or she could get up, put on her dressing gown and go downstairs and clear the dining table.

'Daisy.'

Damn. Too slow.

She looked up, her eyes lingering on his body, making an inventory, storing up the memories. This wouldn't happen again. She knew that. He was about to tell her that, just as soon as he'd pulled on his clothes and that beautiful, perfectly honed body was hidden from her eyes.

Or partly. Dressed only in the jeans, he sat on the edge of the bed and took her hand, pulling it away from its death-grip on the quilt and folding it inside his own.

Here we go, she thought. *The gentle put-down.*

'That was incredible,' he said softly. 'And I want to stay, to make love to you all night, but it isn't going to happen. It can't happen. I'm going home to get a decent night's sleep, and in the morning we'll go to work and act as if nothing's changed, and then afterwards we'll talk about it, OK?'

She swallowed. 'It's OK, Ben, I know it was a mistake.'

His thumb stroked her wrist. 'It was, but we've done it now, and it's changed things, and I don't think we can really just put them back the way they were. We have to find a way to move forwards from this.'

She nodded. They did, but she couldn't imagine how. She didn't know what she wanted, she just knew nothing so special had ever happened to her and she was in no way finished with it, but of course nothing had really changed. It was just different, but it still had no future, and a feeling of impending loss settled over her.

'We'll talk tomorrow,' she agreed. 'I'll cook for you.'

'No. It's Friday tomorrow, isn't it? Damn. I'm at Jane's with Florence, and Jane might have plans to go out. It'll have to be Sunday night, after I've put Florence to bed and come home. We can get a takeaway or something.'

'I can cook, you know,' she said, finding a smile from somewhere.

He smiled back, his eyes troubled and yet tender. 'I'm sure you can. Don't go to a lot of trouble, I don't know how late I'll be. Jane's away for the weekend and I can't leave till she's back.' He sighed softly. 'I have to go now, it's getting really late and if I don't leave I'll end up staying and I don't think that's a good idea, but I'll see you in the morning. Maybe we can grab a coffee.'

He leant over and kissed her, his lips tender and lingering, and then he straightened up, gave her a tiny, slightly sad little smile and then went out, and she lay and listened as he closed her front door behind himself, opened his own, went up the stairs and into his bedroom.

She heard him moving around, then he went still, and she could swear she could hear him breathing on the other side of the wall.

'Goodnight, Daisy,' he said, his voice soft but clear in the quiet.

She didn't answer. She was too busy wondering what the future held. She didn't have a clue, but she was pretty sure she wouldn't like it…

They didn't have time for a coffee on Friday morning, and they didn't have time for lunch, either.

He disappeared off her radar that afternoon to see Florence and reappeared on Sunday night at seven, by which time she'd had plenty of opportunities to think about their relationship and where it was going. And she'd come to exactly no conclusions.

'You look bushed,' she said, letting him in, and he gave a tired laugh and hugged her.

'I am. Florence was exhausted, too, that's why I'm so early. We've had a busy weekend, and she crashed at six, and Jane was back so I thought I'd get away.' He sniffed the air and smiled. 'Something smells tasty.'

'I made a casserole. I just have to heat it up when we're ready.'

'Great. Stick it on now, I'm ravenous. And then maybe we can talk.'

They needed to. There was no way she'd intended to go to bed with him on Thursday night—or any other night, come to that. Her boss, her neighbour—and another divorced father? No way. But that night—that night had been something she'd had no defences against, and she didn't think he had, either, thinking back. And she'd had all weekend to do that.

What to do?

'OK, fire away,' she said after she'd switched the heat on under the casserole.

'You aren't going to make it easy, are you?' he said wryly, meeting the challenge in her eyes.

'I need to know, Ben,' she said softly. 'I need to know where I stand with you. I know we shouldn't have done it, but as you said, we have now. So where do we go from here? I haven't got a clue.'

'I don't know. I've been thinking about it all

weekend, and I wondered—maybe if we had some kind of framework,' he suggested.

'What—like rules?'

He felt himself frown. 'I don't like the word rules. Parameters, maybe.'

'Such as?' she asked, trying to be rational because the idea of never holding him again was hard to take, however sensible it might be.

'Separate compartments,' he said honestly. 'I have to keep Florence out of my private life, for everybody's sake. You won't ever see her—well, not in any relationship context, anyway. As far as Florence is concerned, you'll be my neighbour. That's all. The lady next door. Not Aunty Daisy. But she isn't what this is all about. This is about two consenting adults who've both been hurt in the past, having a relationship with clearly understood boundaries, and Florence doesn't come into it at all.'

She was relieved about that, but in another way gutted, because there was a quantum leap from what he was offering her now and the way she was starting to feel about him. That little flicker of hope that maybe, finally, her luck was changing.

Stupid. She knew perfectly well it wasn't. They'd talked about that, about the fact it was going nowhere, long before they'd scrambled their brains and ended up in bed.

'So what are you suggesting?' she asked a little warily. 'We just—' she shrugged '—carry on?'

'If you feel we can. But I don't want anyone knowing about it at work. Not about this. I want them kept utterly separate, to protect both of us when—'

He left it hanging, but she knew what he was saying. When it came to an end, which it would. Of course it would. But maybe not for years. She was only twenty nine. She could afford to take time out to dally with a man who made her feel like no man had ever made her feel before, but not an indefinite amount unless she wanted to give up all hope of having a family of her own one day. And Ben—well, Ben hadn't wanted this. Not with her. Too messy, in so many ways.

Oh, lord. It was all her fault. If only she hadn't kissed him. If only she'd kept her hands to herself, not held them out to him in that blatant invitation—

She shut her eyes. 'I'm sorry. I shouldn't have taken you upstairs.'

'Let's not play the blame game, Daisy,' he said softly. 'I kissed you first, on Monday night. I couldn't help it. And I couldn't help it on Thursday either. I needed you, and I think you needed me. And we still do. Well, I do, anyway. And it *is* about more than just sex, much more, but we can't let it grow into anything dangerous. You just have to understand that this can never be anything other than what we had the other night, no matter how amazing it was. If you can accept that, then we can carry on.'

'As what? Lovers?'

He shrugged. 'If you like. Lovers, friends. It would give us someone to do things with—have dinner, go to the cinema, chill out in front of the telly—just ordinary stuff, but not alone. I'm sick of being alone, Daisy, of having no one to share things with, nobody to tell a joke to or unload on at the end of a rough day. And I would very, very much like to do that with you, but it's your call. If you tell me to go to hell, I'll quite understand, and you don't need to be afraid that it'll affect our relationship at work. I wouldn't do that to you.'

She held his eyes, saw the regret, the need, the sadness, and felt her eyes fill. She was lonely, too, and having someone to share the little things with would be wonderful.

And even though she knew it was the stupidest thing in the world, the last thing she should be doing, she nodded.

'OK. But only so long as Florence is right out of the picture. I can't lose my heart to another little girl, Ben. I've done it before, and I swore never again. Mike's girls came to us every other weekend, and for holidays. And when he went back to his ex, I lost contact with them. And I vowed never again—not a man with children.'

'Oh, Daisy, I'm sorry,' he said softly. He could see the hurt in her eyes, the wariness, the soul-deep pain the breakup had caused her. 'I had no idea you were in so deep.'

'Oh, yeah,' she said with a brittle laugh. 'So if we're going to do this, well, just keep her away from me, please.'

'I will. So—do we have a deal?'

'What—fun dates, hot sex and no complications?'

He winced. 'Daisy, don't,' he said softly, but she wasn't in the mood to be toyed with.

'It's the truth, Ben. If we can't have anything else, then let's for God's sake have that.'

'OK,' he said softly, after a silence that had stretched on altogether too long. 'Fun dates, hot sex and no complications. And one more rule. No using the "L" word.'

She swallowed, nodded, then tried to smile. 'Done,' she said. 'So—is eating a complication, or a fun date? Because I'm starving and that casserole must be warmed through by now.'

He started to laugh, then pulled her gently into his arms and hugged her close. 'Oh, Daisy. I'm starving, too, and it smells fantastic. Actually, I've got an idea. Can we take it with us next door? I've got one or two things I have to do, and I've got a nice bottle of wine in the fridge and half an apple pie.'

'Home-made?'

He winced. 'Yes. By me and Florence, so it's not amazingly elegant, but it's tasty.'

She smiled at him. 'Tasty sounds good. Lead the way.'

They ended up in his bed.

Not then, not until they'd eaten the casserole on their knees in the sitting room—the only room apart from his bedroom that was in any way in order, if you didn't count the dangling ceiling paper.

He opened the wine he'd had chilling and poured it into champagne flutes, 'All I seem to have left,' he told her wryly, and they toasted his house, and the plumber's health, which made her laugh.

And then, when they'd eaten her casserole and the endearingly inelegant and tasty apple pie, he pulled her to her feet.

'Come to bed,' he said softly, and her breath lodged in her throat as she followed him up the stairs and into his room. He undressed her slowly, his hands sure and gentle, but then she met his eyes and saw the fire blazing in them and realised he was hanging by a thread, holding onto his control so he didn't rush her.

He didn't need to bother, but it was an interesting notion. She returned the favour, unbuttoning his shirt with agonising slowness, driving him to fever pitch. She slid the shirt off his shoulders, and as it fell to the floor, she looked past his shoulder to the bedside table and saw the picture.

A little girl with a tumble of dark curls, a tiny turned-up nose and laughing eyes.

Her father's eyes.

She turned her head back and unfastened his belt, then the stud of his jeans, then the zip, tooth by tooth.

Florence was nothing to do with them. This was about them, not her. Fun dates, hot sex and no complications, remember, Daisy? And absolutely no 'L' word.

Taking care not to look at the photo again, she moved into his arms and lifted up her face to his kiss.

She didn't stay.

'The plumber's coming at seven thirty tomorrow,' he reminded her, 'so I need to empty the airing cupboard and sort some stuff out.'

She wanted him to ask her to stay, wanted to tell him she'd help him sort it out in the morning, they could do it together, but that was crazy, and she was still trying not to let herself fall for him. And she certainly wasn't going to beg for crumbs.

'That's fine, I've got things to do as well. Feel free to use my bathroom while yours is out of action,' she offered instead, and he nodded his thanks and dropped a slow, lingering kiss on her lips as she left.

'No, no, no,' he groaned, dragging himself away. 'I have to get on. I'll see you tomorrow at work.' She nodded, and he kissed her again.

'Sleep tight,' he murmured as he let her out, and she went home and made a cup of tea and took it to bed, reading her book and listening to the sound of him shifting things around next door, emptying the airing cupboard and moving the boxes off the landing, and she lay there and tried not to feel cheated.

'Oh, stop it! You knew the rules,' she reminded herself, and clearly spending the night with her came under the heading of complications. She would soon get used to the routine.

And as routines went, it sounded pretty straight-forward. If she was in, and he was in, they'd see each other. If not, they wouldn't.

Wednesday evenings with Florence, he'd told

her, were utterly sacrosanct, and from Friday to Sunday nights he would have her to stay, once the house was ready, but until then he'd stay with his ex at the weekends, as he had this weekend.

She tried not to imagine them together. It had been plaguing her all weekend, but he said she'd been away, so they couldn't have spent the weekend in a passionate clinch. Unless he'd lied? He'd seemed keen enough to make love to her after supper, but he hadn't wanted her to stay the night, and her old insecurities came back to haunt her.

Was monogamy one of the rules?

Not that she was about to ask, but it was hard telling herself it was none of her business, because for all they had very strict rules, that was surely one of them?

It hadn't been for Mike. He'd been sleeping with his wife off and on the whole time they'd been together, she'd eventually discovered. And he wasn't Mike, she reminded herself fiercely.

Whatever, on Wednesday, Friday and Saturday evenings he'd have Florence, and on all the others he'd be free—free, and ready for some adult conversation and recreation. Especially the recreation, she thought with a twinge of sadness.

And that was all she wanted from him, she reminded herself sharply. No complications, no painful, heartwrenching involvement with little children who'd been so easy to slot into her life. No 'L' word. She didn't want declarations of undying love, like she'd had from Mike, followed by the inevitable excuses and gradually cooling and then the bombshell, just when the children had started calling her Mummy Daisy.

She turned over and thumped the pillow, blinking away the tears. It still hurt so much to think about. Two years! Two years she'd been with him, living with him, giving him everything she had of herself, and he'd thrown it back in her face. And the stupid thing was, she'd *known* something was wrong. She just hadn't known what.

No, she didn't need another relationship like that to suck her dry. Once was enough, for any woman.She propped herself up and looked at the clock. Midnight. Too late to phone Amy in Crete. She'd be back on Wednesday. She'd talk to her then, get a little sensible perspective on it. God knows she could do with some.

And in the meantime, she needed sleep. She

flopped back down onto the pillows, stared at the ceiling and finally drifted off, the picture of Florence on his bedside table haunting her dreams.

CHAPTER FIVE

THE plumber arrived on the dot the next morning, and Daisy bumped into him on her way to the hospital a few minutes later.

'He's got his work cut out with this one,' Steve said, jerking his head towards the house, and she laughed.

'Tell me about it. Look after him for me, won't you, Steve?'

'Like that, is it?'

She rolled her eyes. 'He's my boss. I don't want to be in trouble because my plumber takes the mick out of him with the bill.'

'I wouldn't do that, Daisy, you know that,' he said. 'Besides, the wife's due in a few weeks. Don't want to upset the delivery driver!'

'No, you don't,' she said with a grin, and left him to get on. She met up with Ben in the antenatal clinic later in the day and relayed the conversation.

'I'll get the staff to look out for her. What's her name?'

Daisy shrugged. 'Mrs Steve?' she offered, and he sighed and smiled.

'I'll ask him. With any luck she won't need us. I thought Evan was on with me this afternoon?'

'He was, but he's been called to the labour ward, so he thought you might want me.'

Unfortunate choice of words. She felt herself colour, but Ben just smiled, one eyebrow tweaking a fraction, and stuck to the script.

'Good. Could you give me a hand? It's a bit hectic.'

'Sure.'

She was out in the waiting room calling for her next patient when a woman caught her eye and all her antennae went on red alert. She didn't like the look of her at all.

Pale and sweating, she was obviously in pain, and she was waiting to be assessed when Daisy spotted her. Veering away from her next patient, she asked her who she was, picked up her notes and took her into her room to examine her.

She said she'd come in because she thought she was in labour, but Daisy didn't think she was.

Her abdomen was rigid, her pulse was raised, her blood pressure was falling and even though she had no external signs of bleeding, Daisy had a thoroughly bad feeling about her.

'I'm just going to get Mr Walker to look at you, Debbie,' she said with a smile, and leaving the door open and the midwife in attendance, she went in search of Ben.

'Excuse me, could I borrow you for a moment?' she said calmly, and he turned from his patient and met her eyes.

'Can it wait a minute?'

'I don't think so, no.'

He gave a curt nod and joined her outside the door a moment later, one eyebrow raised in enquiry.

'Placental abruption, 34 weeks,' she said succinctly, and he wasted no time.

'Call Theatre, get Evan in there if he's free yet, if not we'll do it. Where is she?'

'Cubicle 2. Her name's Debbie Haynes.'

She paged Evan, discovered he was still up to his eyes with a tricky delivery and went to tell Ben. By the time she got there Debbie was on a trolley and heading for the lifts, phoning her husband en route, and Ben was with her putting a line in as they moved. He waved her over, and she ran and joined them as the lift doors closed.

'Good call. Can you assist?'

'What about the clinic?'

'It'll run late,' he said candidly.

'OK.' She smiled at the woman. 'It's all right, Debbie, you're in safe hands.'

Normally, it would have been a platitude. This time she meant it—assuming they were in time.

She had a general anaesthetic, because time was of the essence, and even though Daisy thought she'd seen him do a section fast before, it was nothing on this. Like the well-oiled machine that it was, the team had sprung into action at her call and were ready for them. A runner with blood was on the way, a SCBU crib was in the room and an army of neonatal specialists descended on them, just in time to receive the dark, floppy baby from Ben's hands.

He swore softly, but there was no time to worry about the baby when the mother was bleeding out. He dealt with the placenta, then held a pressure pack firmly against the site while the drugs worked to contract her uterus, and gradually her blood pressure picked up.

And then, out of the blue, she arrested.

Ben swore again and looked at Daisy. She had the paddles in her hands already, the pads stuck on, the defibrillator charging.

'Clear,' she said, and he let go of the pressure packs and stepped back. Debbie arched off the table, and their eyes all locked on the monitor.

'OK, we've got her back,' the anaesthetist said, and in the background they heard the thin, mewling cry of a newborn baby.

An audible sigh of relief filled the room as the tension was released.

Ben put the pressure back on and shut his eyes briefly, and when he opened them they were brighter than she'd ever seen them. 'OK, let's make sure this bleeding's sorted and then close,' he said matter-of-factly. 'Sounds like Debbie's got a baby to meet.'

'Well spotted.'

'It was pretty obvious.'

'No. You were observant,' he said, giving praise where it was due—something he was sure Evan didn't bother with. 'She was going downhill fast, and you spotted her in the nick of time. Thank God she had the sense to come to the hospital for a check-up and didn't just wait and see. It saved her life, not to mention the baby's.'

'No, you saved both of them,' she said quietly. 'I've never seen a section done so fast.'

Nor had he. 'It's not the neatest.'

'It didn't need to be neat. It needed to save two lives, and you did it. Thank God you were there. And anyway, it *was* neat. You wouldn't let it be anything else.'

'Rumbled.' He smiled down at her and dropped the last set of notes on top of the pile. 'What are you doing now?' he asked as they left the clinic.

'Going home,' she told him wearily. The clinic was finished—well over time, due to their abrupt departure with the emergency, but that was the nature of obstetrics. Some things—some babies—couldn't wait.

His voice was a low murmur. 'Fancy celebrating?'

'Debbie's baby?'

'Debbie's baby, my first week in a new job—us?'

'I thought there wasn't an "us"?' she said quietly.

'Of course there's an "us".'

There was. Of course there was, he was right, but there wasn't really supposed to be.

'There's a pub in Woodbridge,' he suggested. 'We could try that.'

Rather than go public in their own patch?

'Sounds good,' she said.

'I'll book a table, then. Is it OK if I come round and have a shower before we go out?'

'Of course it is.'

Except they ended up sharing the shower, and he had to call the pub and move their reservation.

They went in his car, which was, of course, a much nicer car than hers, and she guessed he'd had it since before the divorce. She settled back against the leather upholstery and sighed. 'Nice,' she said, and he laughed.

'Yes. Luckily I managed to keep Jane's hands off it. She doesn't like automatics.'

She found herself speculating again about their weekends. Speculating too hard, apparently, because he reached across and took her hand.

'What's the matter?'

'I was just thinking about your wife.'

'Ex-wife. What about her?'

She shrugged. 'I know it's stupid, and it's none of my business, but—when you stay there, at the weekends…'

He slowed abruptly, hitched up on the kerb and cut the engine. 'No way,' he said firmly, sounding appalled. 'Did you seriously imagine—hell, Daisy! You think I'm *sleeping* with her?'

'Well, it wouldn't be that unreasonable, would it?' she said, trying not to let her insecurities show. 'I mean, it's not as if you haven't done it before.'

'Daisy, it's over!' he said, even more firmly, and he took her hand and wrapped it in both of his. 'Jane and I are finished. We hardly even started. We never really loved each other, and the only reason I have anything to do with her is for Florence. Believe me, there is no chance of us ever having anything to do with each other ever again, not in a personal way. Besides, I've got a sneaking suspicion her old flame might be on the scene.'

'Really? Does Florence know?'

'Not as far as I'm aware. She shouldn't. Jane knows that and she's promised she'll keep any relationships discreet. Not that it would be hard, if it is him, because he's in the army and he's away a lot of the time. And trust me, when he is, it's no part of my duties to fill his shoes. I've tried that once before, and Florence was the result.'

'They were still together?'

'No. She was on the rebound from him, and very far from over him. I was there. She got pregnant. End of story.'

Yikes. That was a bit of an info-dump she hadn't expected, and she filed it away to think about later and told herself to relax. 'Sorry. I was just—I mean—we didn't specify anything in the rules about monogamy…'

'Daisy, there aren't any rules!' he said, his thumb grazing the back of her hand gently. 'Not really. We're making it up as we go along, but—absolutely, monogamy is key. I'm not and never have been promiscuous, and I don't intend to start now. You're the best thing that's happened to me for years, and I'm not going to sacrifice what I have with you by revisiting a relationship that was a disaster from start to finish!'

She stared at him, and then started to smile. 'I'm the best thing that's happened to you for years?'

'Without doubt, and with the exception only of Florence. And as you know, she has to come first.'

'Of course she does. I wouldn't want it any other way. I couldn't respect you if you felt any different—and for what it's worth, you're the best thing that's happened to me, too.'

Their eyes locked, and he gave a soft sigh and leaned over and kissed her gently on the lips.

'Bless you,' he said quietly. 'You're a sweetheart. I'm so sorry it can't be more than this. You deserve so much more, and I just can't give it to you, but I'll never lie to you. That much I can give you.'

She touched his cheek. 'That's all I want. I'm not really ready for more yet myself, and I'd rather have this than nothing,' she told him honestly, and wondered how long she'd feel like that. A year? Two? Ten?

Forever?

She felt her future drain away, subjugated to the love of this man, and she straightened up in her seat and looked ahead. Love? Oh, God, no. The 'L' word was banned!

'We'll be late,' she said, and he put the car in

gear and pulled away, while she sat there and contemplated the fact that while she'd been keeping her head focussed on the 'no complications' part of the deal, her heart had apparently had other ideas.

She was in love with him, and it was going nowhere, and all of a sudden she wanted to cry.

Clare Griffiths, their pre-eclampsia patient Ben had delivered on his first day, was improving rapidly and now spent all her days sitting by her little son in SCBU, watching over him as he slowly grew stronger. They bumped into each other in the café on Wednesday, and Clare bought her a coffee.

'Just to say thank you, although it seems a pretty pathetic thank-you for all you did.'

'I didn't do anything special,' Daisy protested, but Clare shook her head.

'It may not have felt special to you, but to me— you just took the time to talk to me, to explain what was happening, and Mr Walker—well, he was brilliant. So quick, so decisive, and I just— well, I felt safe with both of you looking after me, so thank you.'

'My pleasure,' she said, touched by Clare's words. 'I'll pass that on to him.'

'Oh, I've already told him. He thinks you're special, too.'

'Does he?' Daisy was startled, amazed that he'd discussed their private feelings with a patient, but Clare just smiled.

'Oh, yes. He said so. He said he was very lucky to have you working with him, and that you were excellent.'

She felt a little wash of relief. Of course he was praising her and backing her up to the patients. She was a member of his team. What else would he do? But she still felt a little glow of pleasure to know that he'd done it.

'Well, you're looking a lot better than, what— ten days ago?' she said, changing the subject swiftly. Ten? Was that all it was since she'd met Ben? Amazing. 'So, tell me all about Thomas. How's he doing?'

'Really well. Why don't you come and see him on your way back?' she asked, and Daisy hesitated for a second and then folded.

'Do you know what? I'd love to,' she said with a smile, and they walked in to find Ben there, standing by the crib chatting to one of the nurses as he looked down at young Thomas Griffiths with a tender smile on his face. He glanced up as they approached and his smile widened.

'Clare—hi. Hello, Daisy. Come to see Thomas?'

'I have. I thought I'd play hooky for a moment as it's quiet. Is that OK?'

'Of course it's OK. He's looking good, Clare, isn't he?'

'He is. I'm just about to get him out and feed him. Want to give him to me? I know you're itching for a cuddle.'

He chuckled. 'Sit down, I'll get him out for you.'

He snapped on gloves and reached into the incubator, juggling the tubes and wires with careful, gentle hands while the nurse supported their weight, and little Thomas lay there cradled securely, fast asleep in Ben's outspread fingers like a tiny doll.

'There you go, little man,' he murmured. 'Here's Mummy.'

He settled the tiny baby gently in Clare's arms, pausing to run a gentle finger over his soft, transparent cheek, and Daisy felt a huge lump in her throat. She'd seen him in Theatre with slippery little babies in his capable hands, passing them swiftly to the midwife—very swiftly, in Debbie's case. She'd seen him deliver Thomas a little more slowly, but no less carefully. She'd seen him in the delivery rooms wielding the forceps or Ventouse with ludicrous ease and then handing the babies over to their mothers as if it was all in a day's work—which of course it was.

But here he was for no good reason, sneaking a cuddle with little Thomas, his big, strong hands cradling a tiny infant with such exquisite gentleness that she felt her eyes fill.

Was he like this with Florence? Yes, of course he was. He'd be a fantastic father, devoted, patient, gentle—Florence was a lucky little girl.

'He's beautiful, Clare,' she told her softly. She was aching to hold him, but he didn't need over-handling, and besides, they had work to do, so they left her feeding him and headed back to the ward.

'You know she thinks you walk on water,' she said to him as they went, and he chuckled.

'We aim to please,' he said. 'She's looking good, isn't she?'

'Very. And the baby's gorgeous.'

'Utterly. Why do you think I went up there? Although having said that, I think they're all gorgeous. I was talking to Debbie's baby's nurse a minute or so before you came in. He's doing well, too, and she seems to be getting there, thanks to you. He's much stronger than Clare's baby, but even so, that was too close for comfort.'

'So where are you going now?'

'Paperwork—unless there are any deliveries that need me? Any more babies I can legitimately cuddle?'

'You're just a softie under that big tough Yorkshire front, aren't you?' she said to cover her own emotions, and he laughed.

'Absolutely. Why do you think I do the job? Right, I've got a huge pile of paperwork needing my attention, then I'm off to pick up Florence, talking of babies.' He lowered his voice. 'What are you doing later?'

'Nothing. Well, that's a slight exaggeration. I'm on call to the labour ward from nine tomorrow, so I'll probably have an early night. If it's anything like last time, it'll be hellish.'

'I hope not.'

'Don't rely on it. I probably won't get away till late.'

He nodded acknowledgement, then with a rueful grin he headed for the mountain of paperwork in the office, and she went home. Amy was back, and she had so much to tell her. She couldn't believe so much had happened since Laura's hen weekend, and she needed Amy's take on it.

And at some point in the future, she was sure, she'd need Amy's support.

Not that she was going to let herself think about that now. For now, she was happy just to be happy, and when it was over—well, she'd worry about that when the time came.

'Are you home? I've got lots to tell you.'

'Sounds exciting. Bring some food.'

She raided her fridge and freezer, drove round to Amy's house and let herself in, hugging her friend and standing back to look at her.

'Wow, you're brown! So how was Crete? Was it gorgeous?'

'Utterly fabulous. What's in the bag? I'm famished.'

'Pizza and salad.'

'Great. Stick it in the oven and tell me whatever it is you have to tell me. And you can tell me all about the new consultant, as well. Forewarned is forearmed and all that!'

'Ah. Yes, well, it's one and the same thing, really,' she admitted, and Amy's eyes narrowed.

'I'm—um—seeing him?'

'What!'

'Off the record.'

Amy plopped down on a stool at her breakfast bar and gaped. 'So—come on, tell me more! What's he like? And how on earth did this happen?'

'His ceiling fell down?' she offered, and Amy's eyes widened. 'He's also my new neighbour. Did I mention that?'

'No, you damn well didn't! Come on, you can't stop there!'

So she told her—all of it, only keeping back the intimate details because they belonged solely to her and Ben, but leaving Amy in no doubt. And then she delivered the punch line.

'He's got a *daughter*?'

'Yup. That's the catch. She comes first, last

and everything in between. No relationships that involve her, he says he's never getting married again, at least not while she's so vulnerable, and to be honest he sounds so adamant about it I don't think he'll ever go there again. So there we have it—the perfect man, utterly ruined by a disastrous marriage and an even worse divorce, reading between the lines.'

'And you love him.'

She rolled her eyes. 'Oh, God, is it so obvious?'

'Well, to me it is, but you *are* spilling your guts so it's not hard to work out. How does he feel?'

She swallowed. 'He says I'm the best thing to happen to him for years.'

'Except his daughter.'

'Except his daughter. How did you guess? But that's fine. I have no issues with him being a good father. How could I? And anyway, that's not what it's about.'

'No. Well, be careful,' Amy said, and peered past her at the oven. 'So how's the pizza?'

'Doing better than the washing. You might want to stop bullying me for the gory details and press the start button.'

* * *

She didn't get her early night in the end.

She and Amy ended up watching a movie until midnight, and by the time she got home Ben's lights were out and she slipped quietly into the house and went straight to bed.

And of course she overslept, woken only by Ben phoning her to say he'd knocked on her door to use the bathroom but couldn't get an answer and was she at home?

She ran down, tripping over the cat, and limped to the door to let him in. 'Sorry, a friend of mine got back from her holiday yesterday and we ended up watching a movie and I didn't get home till late, and then the cat hijacked the bed so I overslept.'

'So why are you limping?'

'I just fell over her. She has this knack on the stairs.'

'The friend?'

'No, the cat,' she snapped, and he started to laugh, then thought better of it.

'Oh, dear,' he chuckled, and pulled her into his arms. 'You're really not a morning person, are you, sweetheart?' he said, and it was on the tip of her tongue to suggest that if he stayed the night he'd have a better chance of judging that, but she thought better of it. No bickering. That was probably in the rules, too.

'I'll make tea. You shower first,' she told him, letting him go reluctantly, and headed for the kettle, feeding the cat on the way. She could hear him in the shower overhead, and the need to be near him was just too great.

She walked into the bathroom, dropped her pyjamas on the floor and stepped into the cubicle behind him, sliding her arms around his waist and resting her cheek against his back.

Heat shot through him, and he turned, tilting her head up to his and taking her mouth hungrily. How could he want her so fast? One touch, one kiss and he was ready—

'We can't,' he said, dragging his mouth away.

'No time?'

'No condoms.'

She gave an impish smile. 'So we improvise,' she said, and he felt her hand curl round him. The breath whooshed out of him, and he nudged her knees apart, slid his hand up her thigh and found the crucial spot with unerring accuracy. Her eyes widened, her mouth dropped open and he cursed his lack of foresight as she climaxed for him.

'That's just for now,' he promised, and then gritted his teeth and bit down on the groan as she took him over the edge.

The labour ward, as she'd predicted, was hectic.

Amy was working there, and she never called for help unless it was essential, but midway through the morning she paged for assistance.

Daisy found her in a delivery room, with a labouring woman lying on the bed and her partner rubbing her back with a worried expression on his face.

'What's up?' she asked softly.

'The baby's back-to-back, and I can't shift it. Mum's knackered, the baby's big, she's been in labour for hours and I think we might need a more experienced hand. Talk about easing back gently into the job!'

Daisy nodded. She'd used the Ventouse before, but never forceps, and if the baby was very stuck or very high, it might need more than suction to help to shift the head.

'You just want to meet Ben,' she murmured out of earshot, and Amy chuckled.

'Oh, yes. But seriously, we might need him.'

'I'll page him.'

He couldn't have been far away, because he walked in a moment later and winked at her. 'Morning, ladies. What can I do for you?' he asked, and Amy spun round, gave a horrified gasp, stripped off her gloves and fled, leaving Daisy standing there staring after her in astonishment.

'Amy?'

'Amy?'

She turned at the sound of Ben's voice, seeing a much milder version of Amy's shock on his face, and her heart sank. No. This couldn't be the guy who'd broken Amy's heart. Could it?

'Back in a minute,' Ben said to the patient, and they went out into the corridor and stared after her.

'Do you know her?' she asked, dreading the answer, but it wasn't in any way the one she'd expected.

'Yes. She had a relationship with my brother.'

'Your *brother*? So—why did she look at you like that?'

'Because we're identical twins,' he said softly. 'I need to talk to her. Where will she have gone?'

'The emergency stairwell, I'd guess. It's our usual retreat for a crisis.'

'Right. Lead the way—and come with me, if you know her well enough.'

'I do. She's my best friend. And for what it's worth, she's never got over him.'

He said something very quiet and very rude. She'd heard it before, when his ceiling came down—which would indicate the seriousness of this situation and the extent to which he was ruffled.

Not as ruffled as Amy. She was crouched on the bottom step of the stairs, waiting for Daisy, and she sucked in her breath as Ben followed her into the quiet space.

'Amy, it's me, not Matt,' he said softly, and crouching down, he took her hands. 'I'm sorry. I didn't mean to shock you like that. I had no idea you were here or I would have warned you.'

She studied him for a second, and the tension drained out of her, leaving her limp and shaken.

'It's OK, Ben, it's not your fault. It just—I didn't—at first glance I…' She broke off, shook her head. 'It took me by surprise, that's all. I'm OK, really.'

'Are you?' he murmured, and then to Daisy's horror Amy started to cry. Ben swore again and sat down beside her, slinging a solid arm round her and hugging her hard against his side. She burrowed into his chest, and Daisy, helpless, unable to do anything, sat down on the other side of her and waited until Amy's tears stumbled to a halt.

'Sorry,' she mumbled, groping for a tissue in her pocket. Daisy handed her one.

'OK, my love?' she asked softly when Amy had blown her nose and shaken her head as if she was trying to clear it.

She nodded. 'He's—'

'I know. He said.'

She sucked in a shaky breath. 'We ought to get back,' she said. 'My delivery…'

'Don't worry, take your time,' Ben soothed. 'Go and have a cup of tea. We'll find another midwife to help us.'

'No. It's OK, I'll do it. I'd rather. I can't bail on her.'

She got shakily to her feet, and with another hug from Ben, she pulled herself together, swiped the tears from her cheeks and followed them out of the stairwell.

CHAPTER SIX

'IS SHE all right?'

'I think so. I caught up with her later and we talked for a bit. She didn't say a lot—she never does.'

He grunted. 'Nor does Matt. Do you think it's going to be a problem, her working with me?'

'She says not, and I'm inclined to believe her.'

He came up behind her and put his arms round her, resting his chin on her shoulder.

'I think she was just a bit shaken up to see me.' He nuzzled her cheek. 'Do you really want coffee?'

'Not really. I thought you would.' She turned in his arms, fully expecting to see a glint in his eye, but instead there was a curious sadness.

'Do you mind if we just go to bed? It's been a long day.' He'd only just got in, and he'd grabbed something to eat in the hospital, he said, but it was more than that, she sensed.

'Of course I don't mind,' she said softly, going up on tiptoe and kissing him with infinite tenderness.

He stayed that night, making love to her with exquisite care and then holding her in his arms all night, and she wondered if it was something to do with Matt and Amy, or if it was something that had happened with Florence yesterday. They hadn't really had time to talk, and in any case, he never talked about Florence to her.

Sticking to the rules?

Whatever, it was lovely to have him hold her all night, and to wake up in the morning with a crick in her neck from sleeping on his shoulder with his arm round her and her leg wedged between his powerful thighs.

'I need to move,' she whispered, and he opened his eyes and smiled.

'Thank God for that. I think my arm's going to drop off.'

She laughed softly and shifted out of his way, and he rubbed his arm and winced while she stretched her neck out and sighed with relief, then rolled back to him and propped herself up on her elbows.

'Good grief, what a fuss! Are you all done whingeing on about a few pins and needles?' she teased.

He moved faster than a striking cobra. One second she was laughing down at him, the next she was flat on her back with his lean, muscled body sprawled over her and her arms pinned to the bed above her head.

'No! No, I'm sorry, I'm sorry,' she laughed, but he just raised an eyebrow, clamped both her wrists together with one large and inescapable hand and trailed his other hand slowly and tormentingly over her body.

'Too late,' he growled. Last night's thoughtful mood was clearly gone, replaced with a playful lust that was much more in keeping with their rule book, and taking his time, he finished what they'd started.

It was all going like clockwork until the following weekend, when she heard his front door open and close during the course of Saturday morning, and then the sound of little running feet.

It stopped her in her tracks, and she stared at the wall in horror. No. He'd said she wouldn't be here until the house was finished, but it was nothing like ready for Florence to stay, and nor was she! She wasn't prepared, her defences were down, her emotions far too close to the surface. Why hadn't he *warned* her?

And then her phone rang.

'Daisy, hi, it's me. Look, I'm really sorry, I've had to bring Florence back here. Jane's got a migraine and she needs some peace, so I've come to get my walking boots so we can go out for a bit of a yomp in the woods, then we might come back here. I hope we don't disturb you.'

Disturb? 'She's not a virus,' she said sharply, even though she'd been mentally chastising him for not warning her, and then felt evil for bitching at him. 'Sorry. Thanks for the heads up. I'll keep out of your way.'

'OK. We might see you later.'

'No!' she said, but he'd hung up. So what now? Should she go out? Leave the house and come back after dark? 'Oh, don't be ridiculous, she's just a child, she's not poisonous! Get a grip,' she told herself, and finished the pile of ironing, then made some lunch and went out into the garden and started weeding.

She'd been there half an hour when there was

the sound of the back door opening, and Ben's voice saying, 'This is my new garden—or it will be. It's a bit of a jungle.'

'It's very messy,' a childish voice piped, and Daisy's heart turned over. She sounded so like Freya…

'Yes, it is messy, isn't it? Shall we make it tidy?'

'Yes! Me do it, Daddy! Me do it!'

She stayed there, frozen, trowel in hand, listening to the soft rumble of his voice as he talked to Florence. Should she go inside? Say something? Tell him she was there? Or carry on and say nothing? No. He'd hear her then. Would he talk to her?

She stuck the trowel in the ground and brushed off her hands. Maybe she'd just creep inside and pretend—

'Hi.'

She lifted her head and saw Ben leaning over the fence, a tentative half-smile on his face as he searched her eyes. He must be standing on something, she thought, and got stiffly to her feet.

'Hi. How was your walk?'

'Great. We saw lots of bluebells, and a squirrel, and then we had some lunch, and now we're going to clear up the garden. I don't suppose you've got a broom, have you?'

'Sure.'

She found it in the shed and passed it over, waiting for the invitation to meet Florence, hoping it wouldn't come yet longing to see the little girl who was so excitedly helping her daddy clear up the messy garden.

No invitation was forthcoming. Instead he smiled and disappeared behind the fence, and left her standing there staring into space.

'Basket case,' she muttered, heading for the conservatory, and she went inside and put the kettle on. Ten seconds later she got a text from him.

Tea would be nice if you're making one.

She rolled her eyes. Tea, indeed. And no doubt biscuits, and something healthy for Florence. Apple juice? She opened the fridge and found an unopened carton of apple juice, and poured some into a little mug, then made two mugs of tea and put the chocolate biscuits on the tray and took them out.

'Tea's up,' she yelled, and he appeared at the

fence, his little mini-me on his shoulders, both of them grinning happily.

'Daisy, this is Florence. Florence, meet Daisy. She's my neighbour. She has good biscuits.'

Florence giggled and squirmed on his shoulders, and he clamped her legs firmly in his hands and disappeared while Daisy tried to get her breath back and unclamp the hand that was pressed over her mouth.

Why on earth had she done this? She should have refused to make the tea, told him to sling his hook and gone out—or just gone out earlier and let him sort his own broom and refreshments.

He was at her gate, letting himself in and holding Florence by the hand. She had one arm round his leg, which was obviously making walking difficult, but he just went slowly and accommodated her as she giggled and hung on, and Daisy's heart squeezed. She was *so* like him!

'We've decided the garden's a bit much for us,' he said with a wry grin. 'We think it needs a gardener.'

'I think it needs a chainsaw and a gang of landscapers,' she said drily, unfairly angry that he'd had to catch her outside and trap her like this.

'Sounds like a plan, and then we'll have a lovely garden for you, won't we, Florence?'

'I like *this* garden,' Florence said shyly, looking around her with eyes like saucers. 'It's pretty. Look, Daddy, a froggy! Daisy's got a froggy!'

Oh, lord, she was so sweet. Her eyes were like huge blue saucers, and Daisy wanted to scoop her up and hug her. She found her voice.

'Yes, I have, but he's not real.'

He was a hideous little concrete frog she'd found in the flowerbed and been meaning to throw out, but now she was glad she hadn't, because Florence sat down on the path and had an earnest conversation with him that had Daisy desperate to laugh out loud. Either that or cry.

'She's delicious,' she mouthed to Ben, and he nodded, watching her with pride and love in his eyes.

'Froggy wants a biscuit,' she said, and Ben crouched down beside her.

'Does he? He has to say please.'

'Please.'

So 'froggy' had a biscuit, and Ben had a handful, and Daisy watched Florence puggling about in the flowerbed and chatting to the frog and feeding him bits of her biscuit, and she watched Ben watching his little daughter, and all the time she could feel the thin, fragile defences around her heart cracking and crumbling in the gentle onslaught.

'I have to get on, I've got things to do in the house,' she said abruptly. 'Feel free to stay in the garden as long as you like.'

And without another word, she got up and went back inside before the wall around her heart came down in a million pieces...

They disappeared later in the day, and he rang her that night, something he didn't usually do at the weekend.

'Thank you for this afternoon,' he said softly. 'I'm sorry we imposed. I just didn't know what to do with her. I thought the garden would be all right, and it was only when we went out into it I realised how many dangerous things there were out there.'

Namely Florence, as far as she was concerned, with him running a very close second! 'It's fine, don't worry,' she said firmly. 'She was no trouble.'

'But I promised I'd keep her out of your way,

and then we didn't have any milk or any juice for her because I wasn't expecting to be there, and that was really pushing it. I'm sorry. I should have just taken her to the playground or to a café but she was tired after our walk.'

She swallowed. 'Ben, it's all right, it was only the once. She's just a child. It's fine.'

Except she wasn't just a child. She was the flesh and blood of the man she loved with all her heart, and seeing his little daughter made her all the more real. Seeing them together. Seeing the love between them, the way his eyes never left her.

He was a good father. A brilliant father. Loving, caring, thoughtful, aware of the dangers but happy to let her get well and truly grubby and be a real child. When she'd got bored with the frog she'd climbed all over him and sat on his shoulders, peering down into his eyes and laughing, and she wished she'd had a camera to capture the moment.

Silly. It was nothing to do with her. *Florence* was nothing to do with her. And she needed to remember that. She went to the drawer where she kept her sentimental things, and pulled out the photo of Millie and Freya. She stared at it for a long time, wondering how they were, if they were happy, who they were living with. Mike and his wife, still? Or had she thrown him out again so they had a different mummy for the weekends? She stroked her finger lovingly over the image. They'd be older now, three years older, so they'd be nine and seven.

Gosh. How time passed.

She stuck the photo on the front of the fridge under a magnet, so she'd see it every time she made a cup of tea and got the milk out, and it would remind her of all the reasons why she was keeping Florence firmly off limits.

There. Now she'd remember. All she had to do was make sure Ben did.

The house being in chaos was doing his head in. Not just because it was messy, but because it meant he couldn't have Florence there.

And then finally, almost four weeks after the ceiling fell down, the kitchen was plastered, the house rewired and the kitchen could go in.

He couldn't wait. Staying at Jane's every weekend had driven him crazy, and the prospect of doing it for weekend after weekend was intolerable, he thought as he packed and set off there yet again. But he had no choice, not if he wanted to see Florence, and their time together was so short, so fleeting, and she was growing like a weed. Her childhood would be gone in the wink of an eye, and the fact that he was missing so much of it gutted him.

But he missed his home, too, while he was at Jane's. He missed having his own things around him—and he missed spending time with Daisy. And the first thing he did after he had a shower when he got home on Sunday night was to go round and see her.

'God, it's so good to be home and get back to normal,' he said, burying his head in her hair and holding her tight. 'I love her to bits, but Florence can be so demanding, and we had to spend the day out because Jane had a headache again today.'

'Is she ill?'

He laughed and let her go, following her into the sitting room and settling down on the sofa with her in his arms. 'Not really. I'm sure she wasn't feeling great, but I took Florence out for hours so she could rest, and when I got back she was on the phone and looked fine. The moment she saw me she had a relapse, curiously.'

'Looking for sympathy?'

'I don't know what she was looking for, but she won't get it. Not from me, anyway. Not in my job description.'

'So you left.'

'After I'd fed and bathed Florence and put her to bed and read her a story. It was the princess and the frog tonight—again. She's got frogs on the brain now, thanks to you,' he told her, tapping her on the nose.

She smiled. 'Sorry,' she said, although she wasn't sorry for him at all for having such a delicious little daughter, and then she reminded herself that she wasn't going to think about Florence. Hard, when Ben was talking about his precious little mite, but if she wasn't careful she'd end up hurt again.

And more to the point, because she was the most vulnerable one, so might Florence.

'Have you eaten?' she asked him, changing the subject.

He gave a hollow laugh. 'If you count fish fingers and peas.'

'Doesn't sound as if you do.'

'Don't worry, I'm fine. I had lunch.'

'What?'

He shrugged. 'A sandwich?'

'I know you and your sandwiches. You had half a cheese sandwich and a banana on Friday, and I don't think you finished the banana,' she reminded him. 'Fancy scrambled eggs on toast?'

'That would be amazing,' he groaned, and she left him slouched on the sofa while she went to make it. When she came back, he was asleep, but she woke him up to eat it, then cleared away, turned off the television and took him up to bed.

Tabitha was curled up in the middle of it, and gave him a disgusted look as she jumped down and stalked off.

'I don't think she likes me stealing you,' he said with a grin, but Daisy just laughed and hugged him.

'Tough,' she said, lifting her face up to his. 'I've missed you. It's been a long weekend.'

His smile was tender. 'It has. Much too long.'

He tunnelled his fingers through her hair, sighed in contentment and rested his forehead on hers. 'Oh, I'm so tired. Florence was really on

form today. Can I sleep in my clothes, please?'
he asked, and stifled a huge yawn.

She laughed, undressed him and toppled him
into bed, then snuggled in beside him and fell
asleep. It was the first time they'd gone to bed
without making love, and there was something
settled and homely and *right* about it.

And if she hadn't been tired, if it hadn't been
late, if she'd been thinking clearly, it probably
would have worried her. But it didn't. Instead
she curled into his side, her hand over his heart,
and went to sleep.

Clare Griffiths took her baby home that week,
and came to say goodbye. He was still small, but
he was a little fighter and he was a lot bigger than
he had been and the paediatricians were happy
to let him go home.

Ben sneaked a cuddle—a proper one this time,
and it stopped Daisy in her tracks. He looked so
comfortable and at home with Thomas in his
arms, as of course he would. He handled babies
all day, he'd had Florence to practise on, and it
seemed that every time she looked up these days
he had a baby in his arms. Her emotions were in

uproar when he looked up and met her eyes and she thought, *What if that was our baby?*

No! Was she going *mad*? Fun dates, hot sex and no complications, remember? Not *babies*! They were *definitely* a complication!

'Here—he wants to say thank you to you, Daisy,' Ben said with a smile, and passed her the tiny infant.

Oh, heavens. As he'd settled his head in the crook of her arm, his fingers had brushed her breast, and it felt so intimate, so—realistic? As if Thomas was theirs, and he'd handed him over for a feed.

Sudden tears scalded her eyes, and she handed him back, gave Clare a hug and said a hasty good-bye and excused herself, disappearing onto the gynae ward to check the post-ops and make sure they didn't need their pain relief adjusted, but Evan had already done it and she wasn't needed.

Pity. She could have done with a good, solid reason to stay out of Ben's way. He was sneaking up on her blind side and it was all Florence's fault for being so utterly delicious. She'd managed to keep children off her radar since Mike, and the babies at work had been just that—babies at work. But not now. Not since Florence. Now they were real, tiny little children, part of a family, and each and every one seemed to tear a hole in her heart.

Florence, quite by chance, had found the chink in Daisy's armour, and the crack just kept getting wider and wider.

By the next weekend, Steve's wife still hadn't had her baby, and so Ben had a kitchen—or at least enough of it to have Florence to stay. He'd stayed up late on two nights painting her bedroom— nothing special, just a quick coat of emulsion over the wallpaper to freshen it up for now, and some curtains and bedding from the local DIY store, and he showed it off to Daisy when he'd finished on Thursday night.

'So what do you think?'

'Wow! It looks tons better. Well done,' she said, looking around it critically and nodding.

'Do you think she'll like it?'

Daisy just laughed at him softly. 'Of course she'll like it, Ben. It's pink. Little girls all love pink.'

He grinned. 'So the woman in the shop told me.

I asked—just to be sure—and she said I couldn't go wrong with that.'

'You haven't. And the curtains and bedding are lovely.'

'Well, they'll do for now. I looked for something with frogs on, but they were a bit thin on the ground.'

Daisy chuckled. 'Don't worry. I expect she'll grow out of frogs soon.'

He rolled his eyes. 'I live in hope. There's only so many times I can read her *The Princess And The Frog* without losing my marbles, but it makes a change from *Goldilocks*, I suppose.'

Daisy made a mental note to look out for frog books, because Florence's birthday was coming up at the end of June, just a few weeks away— and then she realised what she was doing. Stupid. So stupid.

'What?' Ben asked, looking at her thoughtfully, and she shrugged and smiled.

'Nothing. Just remembered something I have to do,' she lied, and vowed to put frogs and books and little girls right out of her mind before she lost it completely. 'I should go and get on.'

'Really? Can't I talk you into staying? I was

hoping we could look at colour schemes, and maybe have a glass of wine,' he said softly, but his eyes were searching hers, and he was too astute to miss the emotions coursing through her, and he sighed before she could answer.

'Daisy, I'm sorry. I'm making assumptions—taking you for granted. You go, do whatever it is you have to do. I'll see you tomorrow at work.'

So maybe not that astute. He'd realised she didn't want to be there, just not why. Well, that was fine. She didn't need an in-depth analysis of her emotional weaknesses.

She kissed him goodnight—hovered on the brink of changing her mind, but left anyway, and lay in her bed alone and wished she could find it all a little easier to be sensible and keep her distance.

She'd stay out of the way this weekend, she vowed. No going out into the garden if they were there, no listening through the wall to the sound of childish laughter—Florence's and Ben's—and absolutely no impromptu tea-parties with Froggy in attendance.

And maybe—just maybe—she'd get that wall back up again, brick by brick, to keep them out of her heart…

CHAPTER SEVEN

SHE went to London for the weekend. Laura's fiancé was away for his stag weekend, and she invited Daisy down at the last minute. She went, and spent the whole weekend talking weddings and helping Laura make the favours for the tables.

Just what she didn't need, but it was probably better than listening to Florence and Ben through the wall, and he'd got the garden landscapers coming to make a start, as well, so she couldn't even have retreated to the conservatory for peace and quiet.

She got home on Sunday evening, and almost immediately her phone rang.

She wasn't surprised. His lights had been on and he must have heard her come in. And he was always ready to see her on Sunday evenings, after the undiluted conversation of a not-quite-three-year-old. After spending the weekend listening to Laura panic about the wedding, she was more than ready to see him, too.

'Hi, there. Good weekend?' he asked.

'If you like wedding planning,' she said with a laugh. 'What did Florence think of her bedroom?'

'Oh, she loved it. You were all so right about the pink. So, what are you up to? I've got a bottle of wine in the fridge and a seafood paella on the go. Fancy dinner?'

Of course she did. 'Mmm, paella?' she mused out loud, teasing him. 'Are you trying to bribe me, by any chance?'

'I can only hope,' he said softly, and she could tell he was reaching out to her, trying to undo whatever it was he felt he'd done on Thursday night when she'd left him and come home, and she felt guilty for letting him stew. After all, it wasn't his fault she'd been letting herself get ahead of the game.

Into another game entirely, in fact, but not any more.

'It sounds lovely. Give me ten minutes for a shower.'

She went round and walked straight into his arms.

'I've missed you,' he said, gathering her to his chest and hugging her gently.

'I've missed you, too,' she murmured, and went up on tiptoe and kissed him, and he made a soft sound deep in his throat and threaded his fingers through her hair and kissed her back. Endlessly.

'I've been thinking about Tabitha,' he said when they came up for air.

The cat? Well, that was unexpected. 'I'm flattered,' she said drily. 'What about her?'

He chuckled and kissed her nose. 'She's been alone all weekend, and the landscapers have been trashing her playground. She might feel the need of a bit of company and reassurance, and I feel guilty for stealing you, so why don't we take dinner back to yours?'

She smiled at him, amazed at his thoughtfulness towards the cat who'd done nothing but treat him with disdain.

'You do realise if we take anything fishy round there, she'll be all over us for it?' she warned.

'Maybe I'm trying to bribe *her* to like me?' he said with a chuckle, and she grinned.

'Oh, it'll work. She's a hussy—just so long as there's fish on the plate.'

Tabitha thought it was Christmas.

She mugged their plates, was thoroughly

spoiled by Ben and spent the evening with them, snuggled on his lap with her claws in his knee and purring like a diesel engine while Daisy enjoyed having her legs to herself for once, but she didn't get the ultimate reward. There was only so much he was prepared to do to earn Tabitha's love, he said with a smile, and sharing the bed was above and beyond the call of duty, so they shut her out of the bedroom and tuned out her protests.

And yet again, he stayed the night.

He had an interesting case in the antenatal clinic the next afternoon, and he went and tracked Daisy down.

'What do you know about MCMA twins?' he asked, and her eyes widened. He could almost hear the cogs turning and for a second he thought she was going to disappoint him. He should have had more faith.

'OK. MCMA stands for monochorionic mono-amniotic—they're identical twins that split at late embryo stage hence share placenta and both foetal membranes, unlike other twins. They're also known as momo or mono twins.'

'Incidence?'

'Tiny. One in a hundred twin pregnancies, maybe?' she tried. 'Stats aren't my best thing.'

'Complications?'

She was surer on this. 'Cord entanglement or compression, twin to twin transfusion, premature delivery and low birthweight.'

'Management?'

'Aggressive,' she said firmly. 'Close supervision, frequent scans, possibly drug therapy from 20 weeks to reduce the level of amniotic fluid. Inpatient from 28 weeks with aggressive monitoring by Doppler up to three times a day, and daily scans as well at 30 plus weeks? Guessing now, but elective delivery from 32 weeks or as soon as viable in the event of an earlier emergency?'

'Death rate?'

'High.'

'How high?'

'Lord, what is this, an exam?' she said with a wry laugh. 'Very high. Fifty per cent? Much less with aggressive management?'

'Excellent. You passed.' He grinned at her. 'Want to come and see some on a 3D scan? Mum and Dad are waiting for us.'

Her eyes widened and she felt a little leap of professional excitement. 'You've got MCMAs in the clinic?'

'Yup—and I want you to work with me on their care. She's twenty-eight, first pregnancy, 13 weeks' gestation. The first scan wasn't clear, so she's had a 3D ultrasound and the radiologist's just phoned me with the result. I'm just about to give them the news and I thought you might like to be involved as it could be the only time you get to see them in your career.'

'You thought right. Wow. Shouldn't they be re-ferred to a specialist unit, though?'

'What, and give my brother the satisfaction? Not if I can avoid it. Anyway, I've worked with him in the same department.'

She tilted her head on one side and stared at him, confused. 'Your brother?' she asked blankly.

'Matt's a twin specialist.'

'Ah.' It made sense, as they were twins, and ex-plained his choice of twin statistics as a cover for her errand on his first day. 'Well, come on, then, what are we waiting for?' she asked impatiently, and he chuckled and led her into the consulting room, introducing her to the patient and her husband, then he brought up the ultrasound images on his computer and swivelled the monitor so they could see it.

'Right, let's start at the beginning, because I don't know how much you know about twins and I want to make sure you understand the baseline, if you like,' he said, and then while Daisy, knowing what was coming, studied the 3D image on the screen, he explained everything she'd just recapped, but slowly, thoroughly and in great detail and without scaring them half to death. Tricky, considering the statistics and the fact that they'd clearly been doing their research.

'Is that the same thing as momo twins?' Melanie Grieves asked, and Ben nodded.

The colour drained from her face, and she grabbed her husband's hand. 'They could—'

She broke off, and Ben gave them an understanding smile.

'OK, first off, I don't want you to panic. I know you will have been trawling the internet, so let's talk it all through, because the stats can look a bit scary until you break them down.'

'Scary? Half of them *die*!' she said, her voice wobbling, and he shook his head.

'Only if they're not monitored properly to keep an eye on the cords and make sure they're not getting tangled or compressed. The next few weeks are probably the most critical, because there's nothing we can do if they get tangled now, but once they've survived to 20 weeks, we can do more, and with aggressive management the odds of surviving rise considerably.'

He went on to explain the management of her pregnancy in detail, and far from being frightened by the intensive nature of the monitoring, she seemed reassured.

'So—where will I be treated?' she asked.

'This is where you get a choice,' he explained. 'It's up to you whether to want to be treated here, locally, or go to a specialist centre in London, and I won't be in the least offended if you choose to do that. All I can promise is that if you stay here with us, I'll do everything I can to make sure that you end up with two healthy, normal babies at the end of your pregnancy.'

'But if I go to a specialist centre, can they do more?'

'Not necessarily. I was working there until I came here, and I do have a special interest, but obviously they deal with more cases as they're a referral centre. The care, however, wouldn't be any different, I'd make sure of that.'

'So are you as good as the consultant there?' Mr Grieves asked, and Ben chuckled. Daisy, on the sidelines, stifled a smile.

'I would have to say yes, but then I am his older brother, by about a minute,' he told them with a grin, and then shocked her. 'We were monoamniotic twins, and we survived, and that was nearly thirty five years ago. Hence our mutual interest.'

'You're momo twins?' Mrs Grieves said, echoing Daisy's incredulous thoughts, and he nodded.

'Yes—and we'd work closely together on your case, so although he might have a little more experience than me, you have to juggle that against the disruption of being treated away from home. In any case the early part of your care would be here, and I'm sure my brother would be happy to review all the scans if I ask him.'

He let that sink in, then added, 'It's a lot to think about. I want you to be scanned every other week for now, and we'll then scan you weekly from 20 to 28 weeks, then admit you to whichever centre you choose for even closer monitoring. Go and think about it, and let us know your decision in the next few days.'

'I want to stay here,' she said firmly. 'I don't want to travel, and if I'm going to have to be an in-patient for weeks, I don't want it to be miles from my family. And I trust you. You've worked there, your interest in the condition is much more than academic, and as you say, your brother will pass anything new on to you. I'd like you to look after me—if you will? If you think it's safe?'

Ben smiled at her and gave a soft laugh. 'Of course I will, Mrs Grieves, and I don't think you'd be any safer there, but I think you should talk it over with your husband.'

'I don't,' he said instantly. 'If she's happy, I'm happy. If you're confident that you can do it as well as them, and it'll save Mel all that stress of the travelling, then I think it's a much better idea. And thank you for taking the time to be so helpful.'

'My pleasure. Take it steady and get plenty of rest. And if you've got anything else you want to ask, you can talk to me at any time. Just ring up and I'll phone you back as soon as I'm free, or you can make an appointment and come in.

And I'll arrange to have some literature sent to you. I don't want you to feel you're on your own with this. Any questions?'

There were a few, and he answered them patiently and comprehensively without hesitation. He clearly knew his subject, Daisy thought, and she could see the parents relaxing as their confidence in him grew.

He said goodbye and showed them out, and Daisy turned to him with new eyes.

'That's amazing. I can't believe you and Matt were MCMA twins. How early were you?'

'Just over a month. They picked it up on ultrasound at 18 weeks, and Mum was transferred to a specialist centre two months later when we were still both alive and mothballed for weeks. She nearly went nuts, apparently, but she got away with it, and so did we. I guess we were very lucky.'

'Evidently.'

'Anyway, I'd like you to read up on it, and if there's anything you want to know, just yell. I've got all sorts of literature at home. Just remember they may very well die if things go wrong in the next few weeks.'

'That's so sad.'

'It's a fact of twin pregnancy. Everyone thinks it's great, but it's not, it's often complicated and it's always riskier than a singleton pregnancy, but with any luck we'll be able to give them two healthy babies. How do you fancy dinner later?'

She blinked at the change of subject. 'Sounds great, my fridge is empty. What did you have in mind?'

'Fish and chips on the seafront while we watch the sunset?'

She laughed. 'That sounds amazing.'

'I thought so,' he said cockily, and winked. 'Come on, then, pull your weight, Dr Daisy. Haven't you got patients waiting?

The sunset was glorious, and they sat on a bench on the clifftop eating their fish and chips out of the paper while they watched the clouds change colour.

'This was a great idea,' she said as she finished, and leant over and gave him a greasy little kiss on the cheek. He laughed and rubbed it off, then slung his arm round her shoulders and they stayed there, heads together, staring out to sea until the reds and golds faded to the purple and silver of moonlight.

The temperature plummeted as the sun went down and Ben felt her shiver, so reluctantly they strolled back to her house and sat in the conservatory drinking tea while he emailed Matt from his phone about the Grieves twins and she flicked through the literature he'd given her.

'You were so nearly conjoined twins! If the embryo had split any later you would have been,' she said, looking up at him, and he gave a hollow laugh.

'Tell me about it. Damn good job we weren't, we would have killed each other. Close as we are, we're not that close and we're both far too opinionated and independent.'

'It must be so weird to be that close to someone,' she said thoughtfully. 'Snuggled up in the womb, really able to touch each other—odd. It must make a bond like no other.'

'I guess it does,' he said thoughtfully, putting his phone down. 'I don't really think about it and I don't know what it's like to have a normal sibling of a different age. There's only the two of us. I think by the time my mother had got over the shock, she didn't want any more. I think we were a bit of a handful.'

'I'll bet. Did you live in town?'

'No—well, on the edge of town, with fields behind the house, and we had a million rescued cats and dogs and rabbits and goats and God knows else what to keep us occupied.'

'Why weren't you a vet?' she asked curiously, and he laughed.

'Because I didn't want to spend my life up to my knees in mud and worse, freezing to death in a stone barn in January with my arm up the back of a cow. Next question?'

She laughed with him, and then gave it serious thought. 'With Matt, do you hurt when he hurts?'

'Gosh. That's a deep one. Do you mean physically?'

'Whatever.'

He nodded slowly. 'Maybe. I was sick when he had appendicitis. We share a lot—tell each other things we wouldn't tell another living soul. But then, don't all siblings?'

'I don't know, I'm an only child. Mike's kids were close, though, poor little things, and I'm glad they were, because at least they had each other. They didn't deserve what he did to them—to all of us.'

His eyes were sympathetic, and he nodded slowly. 'Is that them, on your fridge?'

'Freya and Millie. Yes. I still miss them. If Mike had been half the father to them that you are to Florence, things would have been fine, but he wasn't, he was weak and self-centred and I should have seen it sooner, then none of us would have been so badly hurt.'

'I'm sorry,' he said softly, and she shrugged and got up, shutting the windows.

'One of those things. It was years ago now—nearly three.'

'And he went back to his wife.'

'Yes. He never really left her. They were still sleeping together, all the time he was with me. I had no idea.'

She saw the realisation in his eyes, the explanation for her insecurity over him staying at Jane's.

'Oh, Daisy. I'm sorry. Was that when you moved away?'

'Yes. I didn't need to hear any more about him, and he started phoning me, sucking up again. Bored, I expect. Time to cut and run.'

'Sounds like it was a good move.'

She turned and looked at him, her eyes sad. 'I thought it would be, but I'm not so sure now. Out of the frying pan and all that.'

He felt sick. She looked defeated, resigned, and he'd done this to her. 'Oh, hell, Daisy, I'm sorry. I shouldn't have let this go so far. It was always going to be too complicated. I'm being selfish.'

'No, you're not. I went into this with my eyes open.'

'No, you didn't. I didn't tell you about Florence until we'd almost slept together.'

'I could have stopped it there,' she said, but they both knew she was lying. It had been too late the moment they set eyes on each other, him covered in plaster, her covered in tea. Their eyes had met and that had been it, and their first kiss and everything that followed it had been inevitable.

He shifted the cat off his lap and stood up. 'Do you want me to go?' he asked, wondering if this was the end, if she was finally coming to her senses and kicking him out, as she probably should have done weeks ago, but she shook her head.

'It's too late, Ben,' she said simply. 'I already love you.'

He felt as if she'd punched him in the solar plexus, and he closed his eyes. 'Daisy, no. Not that.'

'What, the "L" word? I thought we'd agreed on honesty?' She reached out for him, taking his hand and cradling it against her heart. 'I know the rules, Ben, and I'm not trying to change anything. I'm just telling you the truth. I just wish it could be different, less complicated, but it isn't and I don't have the strength to walk away from you now.'

God help him, he didn't have the strength to walk away from her, either. He folded her against his chest, rested his face against her hair and breathed in her fragrance. To hell with the rules.

'For what it's worth, I love you, too,' he admitted softly, his voice gruff with emotion. 'And I wish—'

'I know.' She stepped away. 'Come to bed.'

Their loving was heartbreakingly tender, and when it was over Daisy lay in his arms, silent tears leaking from her eyes.

'Don't cry.'

'I'm not,' she lied, her voice clogged with tears.

'I thought we were being honest.'

'We are.' She squeezed her eyes tight shut and hugged him. 'I'm sorry.'

'Me, too. You deserve so much more.'

'Ben, I don't want more, I want you, and if this is what we have, then I'll treasure it for as long as it lasts. And I know that won't be forever, but let's just enjoy it while we can.'

His arms tightened, and he pressed his lips to her hair and wished—hell, he didn't know what he wished. That she'd never met Mike? Oh, yes—but then she wouldn't be here and he wouldn't have met her. That Florence didn't exist? Impossible to wish that.

That Daisy was her mother?

The ache that gave him in the region of his heart nearly took his breath away.

Steve's wife was admitted the following day in labour, and Amy called for Daisy.

'She's breech and I'm not sure she's going to be able to deliver. Want to try, or do you want to send in the big guns?'

'Ben's on call this week. I'll find him,' she said,

reluctant to take the responsibility. She'd tell him what was going on and hand over, but she didn't want to work with him today, she was still feeling fraught after last night.

She shouldn't have told him she loved him. She should have let sleeping dogs lie, but no, she'd had to confess, and now it seemed they were both in deeper than they'd wanted to be, and their light-hearted affair was turning into an emotional minefield.

He was in his office struggling with paperwork, and he was only too happy to leave it—but he was taking Daisy with him. 'You need the experience,' he said, and she couldn't argue with it, so she went. 'Any idea what kind of breech?' he asked as they walked down the ward.

'No. I haven't seen her. The baby turned last night.'

'Really? That's late. I wonder if I can turn it back.'

'Are you good at it?'

'I'm good at everything—except relationships,' he added quietly, and pushed the door open and ushered her in.

'Hello, Steve. Marian, isn't it? Hi, I'm Ben.' He

shook their hands, and Steve looked relieved to see him.

'Glad it's you, guv,' he said anxiously. 'Can you sort it?'

'I'm sure we can,' he said, snapping on gloves and feeling Marian's abdomen. 'Amy, can I have an update?'

'Slow progress, she's 3 centimetres dilated and that hasn't changed for over an hour. Heartbeat's normal, but labour's just not progressing.'

'Your baby's obviously got a skinny little bottom,' he said with a smile, then asked Daisy to feel the baby's position.

'What do you think?'

'It's a frank breech, I think. I'm sure I can feel at least one foot up by the head.'

'Yes. I can only feel one, but the other one won't be far away. So it's a good position for a natural delivery, or I could try and turn it. How frequent are the contractions?'

'Every five minutes,' Amy said, and they then paused while Marian breathed her way through one.

'It doesn't feel as if it's doing anything,' she

complained afterwards. 'It's not like my other labours.'

'How many babies have you had?'

'This is the fourth—and the last. That's what you get for going on holiday to somewhere uncivilised.'

'It was only Turkey! She was on the pill and got sick,' Steve chipped in.

'It happens,' Ben said wryly, and Daisy frowned. Was that what had happened to Jane?

There was no time to think about it, though, because he was feeling her abdomen again, apologising as he dug his fingers in deeply around her pelvis and flexed them a little. 'I think it might be possible to persuade this youngster to right itself. Want to give it a go?'

'Will it hurt?' Marian asked.

Ben pulled a face. 'Not hurt, exactly. It don't think it'll be very comfortable, but all I want to do is push the top and bottom in opposite directions to try and spin it. The baby often joins in and kicks, and that seems to help. Either it'll work, or it won't, and then we think again. Want to try?' he said, and she nodded.

Without wasting any time, he laid one hand

on the back of the baby's head, the other low down on the other side, and as he pushed and jiggled and coaxed, there was a shift, her abdomen changed shape and Ben's hands followed through as the baby somersaulted into the right position.

He straightened up, grinning, and gave Marian a broad wink.

'There you go. One baby, the right way up, and settling nicely into your pelvis. Go on, down you go, little one,' he said, giving it an encouraging little push, and her eyes widened.

'Oh—gosh—that feels a bit more like it,' she gasped, and grabbed Steve's hand, panting furiously.

Amy was at the business end, and she looked up a minute later. 'OK, Marian, that's lovely, keep breathing. Your waters have broken and you're doing really well.'

Daisy and Ben stayed. Technically they weren't needed, but things had moved on so fast that a second midwife hadn't come yet, so they were there when a squalling baby slithered into Amy's waiting hands, bright red with indignation and screaming the place down.

She laid her on Marian's front as she sagged back against the pillows, laughing and crying and trying to get her breath, and as she stared down, her eyes welled over.

'It's a girl!'

'Of course it's a girl,' Steve said, trying and failing to hang onto his masculine pride as the tears coursed down his cheeks. 'Only a woman would change her mind that late, and then change back again!'

They all laughed, and Daisy leant over for a closer look at the new arrival. She'd stopped crying now and she was staring up, transfixed, into her mother's eyes, and Daisy felt an unexpected lump in her throat.

'Oh, she's lovely. Congratulations,' she said. 'Has she got a name?'

'Yes—Tommy,' Marian said drily, and they all laughed again. 'I didn't let myself get carried away with girls' names, because I just knew she'd be a boy like the others.'

'Apparently not,' Amy said with a smile as she clamped and cut the cord. 'Still, you've got a few days.'

'Oh, it seems wrong not having a name for

her,' Marian said, stroking her baby's face with a gentle finger. 'Who are you, sweetheart, hmm? What's your name? Are you a Katie?'

Another midwife arrived, so they left the little family in their capable hands, trying out names on their daughter.

Outside in the corridor, Ben hesitated.

'Coffee?' he said, but Daisy shook her head. Just watching Marian and Steve with their beautiful little girl gave her a hollow ache inside. She was getting broody, she realised, and that was so, so dangerous. So easy to get lulled into a fantasy world, now the 'L' word was out of the box. She should have kept her mouth shut.

'I've got loads to do—patients waiting. I'll see you later.'

Except it was quiet, for once, and she had altogether too much time to think about Ben and the fact that he loved her, too—and that still, even so, there was no way forward.

CHAPTER EIGHT

THE status quo persisted between them for the next couple of weeks. The landscapers had taken down the fence between them, and that weekend, he'd got Florence as usual.

Which would have been fine, except that it was getting hotter as spring moved towards summer, and Daisy needed to plant her containers. And because it was warm, because the landscapers had carefully pruned the trees and left a shady canopy over part of the garden, Florence was out there with Ben, running around in the fresh air and playing games with him.

Daisy wanted to join in.

Well, no, she didn't. She wanted him to take her away, she corrected herself, but of course he didn't, and Florence, being the delightfully friendly little girl that she was, kept coming over to her with things she'd found—a wood louse, a pretty stone, a flower she'd picked her—endless little visits that scraped away at the sore place in her heart until it bled.

'Can Froggy come to my garden?' she asked after yet another trip to show something off. 'I want him to see it.'

'Sure,' she said, and Florence picked him up, very carefully in case she hurt him, and carried him back to Ben, chattering to him all the way.

Daisy turned her back on it all and carried on potting up her containers, but all the time her ears were tuned to the sound of their voices, and she reached for the last pot with an element of desperation.

Thank goodness for that, she thought as she crammed in the last scrap of lobelia and picked up the hose. A good soaking and they'd be done and she could go back inside and make herself scarce.

'They's very pretty!'

She turned the hose off and smiled down at Florence. 'Thank you. They'll be prettier when all the flowers come out, and some of them will smell lovely.'

Her chubby little fingers touched a blue

brachyscome flower with exaggerated care. 'Is that a daisy like you?'

She laughed softly. 'Sort of. It's called a Swan River daisy, and these are verbena, and this is a geranium. Here, squash this leaf in your fingers and smell them. You have to rub your fingers together—there. Can you smell it now?'

Her little button nose wrinkled, and she giggled. 'It smells funny—like lemons!'

'That's right. It's called a lemon-scented geranium, and it has really pretty pink flowers like your bedroom.'

'And the daisies are blue.'

'They are. And the verbena's going to be a lovely purple colour.'

She fingered another plant. 'What's this?'

'That's lobelia, and this is an ivy-leaf geranium, and this is called Creeping Jenny—'

'Daisy, I'm so, so sorry, I had to take a phone call,' Ben said, reappearing beside them. 'Florence, come on, darling, leave Daisy alone. You can see she's busy.'

'No, she's finished!' Florence said. 'Aren't you?'

Her little face was tilted earnestly up to

Daisy's, and she felt her heart squeeze. 'Yes, I am. It's OK, Ben.'

But it wasn't. Her heart was being invaded by him and his little daughter, slowly but surely taking up residence in every nook and cranny of it until it was bursting with love for them.

She looked down again, and Florence was stroking the flowers in the last little pot tenderly.

Oh, what the hell, she thought, and bent down, pressing her hands between her knees and smiling at the little girl.

'I tell you what, why don't you have this little one, and you can water it when you're here at the weekends, and look after it and watch it grow. I'm sure Daddy can find a place for it in your garden somewhere.'

She lifted it up and held it out to him, and after a second's hesitation, he took it.

'Thank you,' he murmured, as if he knew what it had cost her, that it wasn't the plant she was giving his daughter but a gift infinitely more precious. 'There, Florence. Your own pot! What do you say?'

'Thank you,' she piped, beaming at it and then

at Daisy, making her heart turn over. 'Can Froggy look after it for me when I'm not here?'

Ben sighed. 'No, he belongs to Daisy, Florence, you know that.'

'She can have him. That's fine.'

He gave a rueful chuckle and thanked her. She knew perfectly well that he thought the little concrete frog was as hideous as she did, but Florence adored him, and that was all that mattered.

He put the pot down in his garden, out of the way of the landscapers, and she put Froggy down beside it.

'Come on, Florence, time to wash your hands. We're going to go to the playground now.'

Florence ran to the outside tap and turned it on carefully, running her fingers under the dribble. 'Washed them!' she said, wiping them on her once-pink dungarees, and then bent over, sticking her little rump in the air and telling Froggy very seriously to look after her plant. Daisy watched her, torn between laughter and tears, and she was very much afraid the tears would win.

She'd just managed to suppress them both when Florence straightened up and bounced over to Ben and said, 'Ready!'

She waggled her fingers at Daisy, and she waggled hers back and squashed the little pang inside. 'Have a lovely time,' she said, wishing she was going, too. Wishing so many things that were just so dangerous to wish…

Ben, watching the interchange between them, saw the sadness in her eyes just before she masked it, and before he could stop himself, he said impulsively, 'Why don't you come, too?'

'Oh, yes, Daisy come! Please come!' Florence squealed, bouncing up and down with her little curls flying, and he watched the brief internal battle before she crumpled.

She looked up at him, reproach in her eyes, and was on the point of refusing when Florence ran up to her and took her hand. 'Please come? It will be much funner if you're there and you said you're finished,' she begged with wide, pleading eyes just so like Ben's it hurt, and Daisy gave up.

'I'm not dressed for it,' she said a little desperately, but Florence didn't care.

'You can change,' she said with three-year-old logic. 'We'll wait for you. Please please please *please*?'

Cursing him silently, she stripped off her gardening gloves and ran upstairs, changing into clean jeans and a T-shirt. She caught sight of herself in the mirror and was reaching for the makeup when she stopped herself.

No! They were taking the child to the playground, against her better judgement, and she didn't need to tart herself up for it! The sooner they went, the sooner they'd be back, and the sooner it would be over. She ran back down, and found Florence and Froggy in earnest conversation about the plant.

'I'm sorry,' Ben said softly as she reached his side.

She made a small, 'just you wait' sort of noise, and fell in beside them as they headed to the little park just a couple of streets away, Florence dancing around between them like a puppy, oblivious to the atmosphere between the adults.

'Can we go on the see-saw?' she asked Ben hopefully.

'Maybe, if Daisy doesn't mind.'

Daisy did mind, but there wasn't a lot she could do about it. The problem was that although Ben weighed more than she and Florence put together, he was much, much heavier than Florence alone, so without Daisy to balance they didn't have a hope of making the see-saw work.

Simple ergonomics—except there was nothing simple about this equation.

Ben + Florence + Daisy = Disaster, she thought, and she was right. He went on one end, and she went on the other, with Florence cuddled up against her tummy and hanging onto the handle. He sat down carefully, and they lifted up into the air, but not so far that Daisy's feet were off the ground.

And Florence loved it.

Up and down, up and down, faster and faster while Florence shrieked with delight, her little body snuggled safe against Daisy's and making her want to cry. So sweet. So precious. So very, very easy to love.

She could have scooped her up and cuddled her to bits, but she kept on pushing, up and down, and up and down, until finally Ben stopped the ride by bracing his legs and bringing them to a halt.

'More!' Florence pleaded, but in the middle of laughing with Florence and having fun, Ben had caught Daisy's eyes and seen the pain in them, and he'd felt gutted.

What the hell were they doing? What on earth was he doing to her? To Florence? To all of them? He'd promised Daisy he'd keep Florence out of her way, and he'd done nothing of the sort.

'No, that's enough see-sawing,' he said firmly but gently, and got off. 'Come on, I'll push you on the swing. You like that.'

He lifted her clear of the see-saw and carried her to the swings, settling her in the seat safely before pushing it high. The see-saw forgotten, she shrieked with delighted laughter, and Daisy went over to a bench and sat down and watched them, wondering how on earth she could have got herself into this position again.

'I'm sorry.'

He'd lifted her out of the swing and left her on a bouncy little rocking horse nearby, and he sat down heavily beside Daisy and propped his elbows on his knees, his hands dangling between them, looking the picture of dejection. 'I should have thought before I opened my mouth.'

'Yes, you should. You shouldn't have asked me in front of her,' she said quietly. 'You knew I'd have no choice. I couldn't refuse a child, could I? Not without sounding mean.'

He tilted his head so he could see her, his eyes searching. 'You could have done—but I didn't think you wanted to. You looked so sad—as if you couldn't bear to be left out.'

'And this helps?' she asked incredulously. 'I can't *do* it, Ben. It was supposed to be about us— about fun, remember? Fun dates, hot sex and no complications, that's what we said. But it's not fun any more, Ben, it just hurts. I'm sorry. I thought we could keep this in its box, but we can't. It just spills over into everything else, and we're all going to end up hurt. It's just hopeless. You can't keep her away from me while you're living next door, it just isn't possible, and I'm not playing happy families all over again. I'm not ready for this, and I don't know if I ever will be.'

His eyes met hers, the naked emotion in them tearing through her, and then he masked it and sat up straight, his hands braced on his knees as he dragged in a deep breath. 'So where does that leave us?' he asked, dreading her answer, and she gave a sad little shrug.

'We both know it's going nowhere, so why drag it on?'

He opened his mouth, closed it and pressed his lips into a firm line. How could he have been so stupid? It was never going to work. She was on the rebound, he'd known that, and this was resurrecting all that old hurt. Well, he couldn't say he hadn't been warned.

'You're right. I'm sorry. Look, why don't you head on back, and I'll bring her back in a little while. And we'll keep out of your way.'

She nodded and got unsteadily to her feet, then with a little wave to Florence, she walked away.

Something she should have done weeks ago...

'Daddy, why's Daisy going?'

Ben could hardly answer her. The lump in his throat was huge, and he swallowed hard, then again.

'Uh—she's got lots to do,' he said eventually, and wondered if it was his imagination or if his voice really sounded as if he'd swallowed a hand-ful of rusty nails.

'Can I go on the slide?'

'OK. Come on, then.'

He helped her up, over and over again, dredging up a smile from somewhere until he thought his face would crack, then he called a halt and took hold of her hand.

'Come on, let's go back now. It's time for supper.'

'Can we see Daisy?'

'Daisy's busy,' he said, his voice catching, and he cleared his throat and headed for the gate, Florence in tow. He wasn't really concentrating on Florence, just putting one foot in front of the other, his thoughts tumbling in free-fall.

We both know it's going nowhere.

But he needed her so much, and it seemed to have been going so well. For the first time in years, he'd been truly happy.

'Daddy, look at me!'

She was walking along the top of a little low garden wall—something that under normal circumstances he would have stopped her doing, but he just smiled absently and tightened his grip on her hand in case she toppled.

And then a loose brick twisted away under her foot, and she fell off the wall and he jerked her arm up without thinking to steady her.

The thin scream cut through him to the bone, and he dropped to his knees beside her, gathering her gently into his arms as a sickening wave of guilt rushed over him. 'No! Don't touch!' she screamed, backing away, her arm hanging awkwardly in front of her, held in place by the other one, and he stared at her, shock holding him rigid for a second.

He'd dislocated her elbow! He couldn't believe he'd done it. So easy, so stupid. And he knew what to do now, but he couldn't do it alone, and she was his daughter, for heaven's sake, and if he'd only been paying attention…

'It's OK, sweetheart. It's just in a crick. It'll be fine soon. I'll call Daisy, she'll come and help us.' It would have to be Daisy, because Jane was away with Peter. Of all the weekends to decide to go away with him…

He fumbled for his phone, his fingers shaking so much he could scarcely operate it, and when it went straight to her voicemail he could have wept. He was about to call the house phone when she rang him back.

'Ben, I—'

'Daisy, help. She fell off the wall and I grabbed

her, and I've dislocated her elbow, and Jane's away, so I can't ask her.'

There was a fraction of a second of silence, in which she must have heard Daisy sobbing, then she said, calmly and firmly, 'OK, stay with her, I'll bring the car and we'll take her to A and E. Where are you?'

'Um…' He looked around. 'Just—just at the end of the road. We're nearly home, but I can't carry her, she won't let me touch her. Daisy, I can't—'

'It's OK. I'll be with you. Don't move.'

It probably only took her a couple of minutes, but it felt like forever. He thought he was going to throw up, and he couldn't stop shaking. 'Florence, darling, I'm so sorry—come here. Sit on my knee and wait for Daisy.'

She sat, leaning her shoulder against his chest and holding her arm very, very still, the quiet sobbing more telling than any screaming would have been. She was shaking like a leaf, her tiny body racked with tremors, and guilt was crippling him.

If only he'd been paying attention, he would have seen the state of the wall and stopped her before she'd hurt herself. She shouldn't have been on it anyway, it didn't belong to them and he would never normally have let her walk on it—so why had he? Because he'd been selfishly obsessing.

'Ben?'

He lifted his head, and saw Daisy crouched in front of him, her eyes concerned. She lifted a hand and touched his cheek, then stroked Florence's hair gently. 'Come on, darling, let's get you and Daddy to hospital so they can make your arm better. OK?'

Florence shook her head. 'Don't want to go to hospital,' she sobbed unevenly. 'Want to see Froggy!'

Oh, no. Daisy's heart contracted, and she stroked the child's hair with all the love she'd been suppressing for weeks. 'You can come back and tell him all about it very soon. You don't want to make him worried, do you?'

She had no idea if she was saying the right thing or not—not, probably, but if it got her in the car then she'd worry about it later, and frankly Ben looked as if he was past coping with this situation.

'Come on, poppet,' she murmured, helping her to her feet, and then she lifted her incredibly carefully into the car on his lap, shut the door and went round to the front and drove to the hospital as if she was on eggshells.

She let them out at the A and E entrance, then parked the car and ran back.

She could hear Florence sobbing quietly, hear Ben's gruff, tender voice trying to reassure her, and she went in and crouched down beside them.

'Have you checked in?' she asked, and he nodded. 'I'll go and find someone,' she said, and opened the curtain as Andy Gallagher walked up.

'Daisy, hi.'

Thank goodness. She'd met him on several occasions over emergency patients, and he was brilliant. She smiled in relief.

'Hi. Can you take a look at Ben Walker's daughter? She's got a radial subluxation. She fell off a wall and he caught her.'

'Ah,' he said softly, smiled at her, and followed the sound of sobbing.

'Hi, Ben,' he said, and crouched down in front of them. 'Hello, young lady. Who are you?'

'F-Fl-Florence,' she said, sniffing and sobbing.

'Well, Florence, I'm Andy, and I work with your daddy and Daisy here in the hospital. And Daisy tells me you've hurt your arm. Can you show me where it hurts?'

She sniffed again, let go very carefully and pointed to her elbow region.

'Oh, dear. That's not very nice. Shall we fix it, then?' he asked, warning Ben, and taking her elbow firmly in his left hand, he took her hand in his right and with a quick twist and flex, it was done.

There was an audible click, Florence sobbed hysterically for a second or two, then whimpered for a moment before she got off Ben's knee and ran to Daisy, throwing her arms round her shaking legs and hugging her tight.

'Fixed, I think,' Andy said with a smile at Daisy, and Ben shut his eyes, dropped his head back and went chalk white.

'Oh, no, you don't,' Andy said, grabbing Ben's head and dragging it forward over his knees.

A long moment later he straightened up, blinked and pulled a face, and then shook his head. 'Sorry, it's just the shock. I just can't believe I was so stupid. One minute she was on this wall, the next she was screaming in a heap, and it's all my fault.'

'Rubbish, it's easily done. She's fine now. We'd probably better have another look at it, maybe take a picture. Can we do that, Florence? Can we take a picture of your arm?'

'For Mummy?' she asked.

'Oh, God,' Ben said faintly in the background, the implications dawning on him, and Daisy took over.

'It's a picture of the inside—it's very clever. It shows all your bones.'

'Does it hurt?' Her little chin wobbled, and Daisy smiled.

'No. It doesn't hurt at all. It's just like having your picture taken, but you have to keep very still so it doesn't go all blurry.'

'Will you come with me?'

'No, Daddy wants to,' she said firmly, handing responsibility back to her father. He got to his feet and held out his hand to her, then thought better of it and picked her up, cradling her in his arms for safety.

'I'm going to buy her toddler reins so I don't

have to hold her hand ever again,' he growled, and Andy chuckled softly.

'Don't beat yourself up. You aren't the first, and you won't be the last, but you will need to be careful for six weeks or so until it's completely recovered, and it may well recur.'

'Fabulous. That's going to take some explaining to her mother,' he muttered, and they went off to X-Ray clutching the form.

'So how come you're here? Have we got a maternity case in that I don't know about or are you switching specialties?' Andy asked.

'No, I live round the corner from the park where they'd been playing—we're neighbours. I gave him a lift. It was just lucky I was around,' she explained glibly, feeling a twinge of guilt for lying.

'Yes, driving her would have been tricky. Can you take them home?'

'Of course I can.'

Even though I'm not supposed to be having anything to do with them, she thought wryly.

Why did *nothing* go according to plan?

'I want Froggy,' Florence said as soon as they got back. She'd been saying it all the way home, but the last thing he wanted to do was give her the heavy little concrete frog to cradle in her recently dislocated arm.

Ben sighed. He was at his wits' end, exhausted with the emotional roller-coaster of the afternoon, and he just wanted to crawl into a corner.

'Froggy's gone to sleep,' he said softly, 'and it's time you did, too. Come on, let's give you a bath and put you to bed.'

The bath was a nightmare. Lifting her in and out suddenly became fraught with danger, and he gripped her firmly under the arms and hoisted her out, wrapping her in a huge, fluffy towel and snuggling her dry on his lap. The arm was tender, although he couldn't see any swelling or bruising, but when he patted it carefully dry she pulled it away.

'I want Froggy,' she said again, and started to cry.

He should just go out and get it—it was in his garden, he remembered, guarding the little planted pot that Daisy had given her.

His dearest, darling Daisy. Only not his Daisy any more, apparently, because he'd pushed her too hard and he'd blown it.

Pain washed through him, and he crushed it ruthlessly. This was all his fault. He shouldn't have asked her to go with them.

He was dressing Florence and still debating getting the frog in from the garden when he heard her voice call softly from the bottom of the stairs.

'Ben? Can I come up?' she said, and he swallowed hard. She must have come in through the back door from the garden, he realised.

'Sure. We're in the bathroom. Hang on.'

He moved the soggy towel from in front of the door and opened it, to find her standing there with a carrier bag.

'I got these for her for her birthday,' she said in a quiet undertone, 'but I wondered if she should have them now. It's a frog cushion and a story book. I thought, she's had a rough day…'

Hadn't they all?

'Daisy, that's so kind,' he said, feeling choked, and Florence appeared at his side and gave her a wobbly smile.

'Daddy says I can't see Froggy's 'cos he's sleeping,' she said, and the smile wobbled a little more.

Daisy's smile wobbled, too. She crouched down so her head was on the same level, and delved into the bag. 'I know, but I've brought you something else instead—it's a froggy cushion, look. You can rest your sore arm on it while Daddy reads to you, because there's a Freddie Frog book, too.'

Her eyes lit up, and she cuddled the small pink and green cushion to her chest and eyed the book.

'Daisy read it.'

For a second he thought she was going to refuse, but then he saw resignation settle over her, and she held out her hand to Florence and led her back to her bedroom.

'All right, then. Just this once, because of your arm.'

She tucked her in, rested her arm on the cushion, then sat down beside her pillow so Florence could see the pictures. And then she started to read.

'Once upon a time…'

Ben sat quietly down on the other bed, and listened to her soft, musical voice telling the story.

The cushion seemed to be doing the trick, Daisy thought, and she'd snuggled down, the painkillers making her sleepy, and insisted a little tearfully that Daisy read the book again. Common sense would have stopped her, if she'd had any, but she'd given up the unequal struggle, and so she read it again, while Ben sat on the other bed and listened, tears in his eyes, his face drawn.

Then at last her eyes drifted shut, and after another page, Daisy put the book down and tiptoed out. Ben followed, leaving the door ajar, and they went downstairs.

'I'm so sorry. It's been a hell of a day.'

They were standing in the hall, both of them a little uncertain because they had no established protocol for this. A few short hours ago, she'd broken off her relationship with him, supposedly, and yet here they were, hovering midway between the sitting room door and the back door, and all she wanted was to get away.

She didn't think Ben was enjoying it any more than she was. He still looked awful, and he was apologising?

'Don't,' she said softly. 'It's not your fault, it's fine.'

'No, it's not, and nor are you,' he said quietly. 'I've asked far too much of you, and you've just done it without a murmur. I don't know how to thank you.'

'I took you to the hospital, Ben, that was all.'

'I'm not talking about that. Well, I am, but I meant much more. All the endless kindnesses—the silly things. Mopping up my floor on the first day. Getting me the plumber. Getting my suit cleaned. Letting me trash your garden while they change the fence. The pot for Florence. Just being there for me, sharing the downtime on bad days when things have gone wrong, sharing the good times. Just sharing everything without question. Letting me into your life and asking for nothing back. And the cushion and book for Florence—it must have taken you hours to find them.'

'No. There's a craft shop in town, and they had the cushion in the window. The book was in the charity shop next door, it's not even new, but it had Florence written all over it. And tonight seemed like a good time to give it to her.'

'It was. It was an amazing time to give it to her. Thank you for being so thoughtful.' He dragged his hand over his face, and when he dropped it to his side, his eyes were bright. 'You're always thoughtful, though, aren't you? Always kind, always willing to put other people first. I don't deserve you, Daisy. You were right today. We can't go on like this. Everything we do makes you unhappy, and I can't bear to see you unhappy.'

'You make me happy,' she said, her voice hollow with pain. 'It's the situation I can't deal with. It's just too dangerous, Ben. Too messy. I'm glad I could help today, and if I can again, please ask, but otherwise—Ben, I really don't want to see Florence again.'

'Or me,' he said rawly.

Or him. Of course it would be easier if she didn't have to see him again, either, but that was too much to ask for, and possibly more than she wanted, sucker that she was for punishment. 'That's not possible,' she said.

'But it would be easier if I didn't live next door. I'll move,' he said heavily. 'I'll get the house finished and put it on the market, and we'll find somewhere else and leave you in peace. Will you be all right with me at work?'

All right? She doubted it, and as for him moving away and leaving her in peace, she knew that would be a long time coming. The move might happen, but the peace? She doubted it. 'I'm sure we'll cope. And I'll move, not you. I'll look for another job—there's bound to be one coming up. And so long as it's in Suffolk, I can still see Amy regularly. And you'll be close to Florence, and you can settle here and build your career. It makes more sense for it to be me.'

His face contorted briefly, and she hesitated at the door, then leaned over, touching a tender, lingering kiss to his lips.

'Goodbye, Ben,' she said softly, and then opened the back door and went out, closing it quietly behind her. She picked her way carefully through the gardens and made it all the way to her sitting room, with the door closed and her face buried in a cushion, before the first sob escaped.

CHAPTER NINE

SHE'D lied, of course. They weren't all right at work.

Oh, they fudged through, but they avoided each other whenever possible, and Amy took her under her wing and comforted her with girly chats and cake when it all got too much.

There were times when they couldn't avoid each other, of course, and in those times it was excruciating.

The antenatal clinics on Mondays were usually safe, which was just as well because after the weekends with Florence running about all over the house and garden, her nerves were fraught anyway.

Every other week, though, they met inevitably over the Grieves and their MCMA twins. The scans showed the babies tangling, then untangling, then tangling again, and at 20 weeks they had a couple of twists in the cords.

'Will they be all right?' Daisy asked, standing next to Ben and trying to concentrate on the almost photographic 3D scan of the tiny little girls, and he shrugged.

'I don't know. I'm going to put her on drugs to limit the fluid. We've got them this far. Another six weeks and they'll be viable—maybe less, at a push. We'll see. But they're both OK so far.'

'So where are we now? Weekly scans?'

'Yes. Weekly till 28, maybe as little as 26, and then I'll admit her. It depends what these two are up to by then. I'm going to play it by ear.'

She nodded. 'Right. Well, unless you need me in the consultation, I've got lots of patients to see still,' she said, desperate to escape from him, and he shrugged.

She didn't want to be with him, he realised, and he could understand that. It was sheer torture being in the same room as her and unable to touch her, unable to look forward to the evening, when they'd be alone and he could take her in his arms and hold her.

God, he missed holding her. Missed everything about her.

'You go, I'll talk to them. I'll let you know if anything changes.'

'OK.'

She went and he closed the door, rested his head against the wall and sucked in a steadying breath.

Bad idea. He could smell her—not perfume, but something more subtle. A hint of her shampoo, perhaps? Whatever, it dragged him straight back to happier times—times when he had the right to bury his head in her hair and breathe in the sweet, fresh scent. Times when she'd trailed it over his face while they were making love, and he'd lie and look up at her and wonder what he'd done to deserve her.

Nothing, was the answer. He'd failed in his marriage, failed to give his daughter the security she deserved, and he'd failed in his promise to keep her away from Daisy—he was a walking disaster area as far as relationships were concerned, and the best thing he could do was keep himself and Florence as far away from her as possible, even if it was too late.

He wrenched the door open and went to find Mr and Mrs Grieves.

* * *

'So what are you wearing to Laura's wedding?' Amy asked her.

She was on call to the labour ward, and she'd just done a Ventouse delivery. They were 'debriefing' over a cup of coffee and a shared slab of sticky gingerbread, and at the mention of the wedding Daisy lost her appetite.

'I don't want to think about it.'

'It's in ten days! You have to think about it!'

She shrugged. 'I don't really feel like going.'

'I know you don't, hon. I don't, either. But she'd be gutted if we didn't go, and she's relying on us. Why don't we go to Cambridge this weekend? Have a properly girly day out together. We haven't done it for ages.'

They hadn't, and Daisy felt a pang of guilt. 'OK,' she said, and then tried to inject a little enthusiasm into her voice, but she couldn't summon any enthusiasm for it.

For anything, really. Without Ben, her life was drained of colour, and she wondered if it would ever be the same again—

'Oh, Daisy. I'm sorry,' Amy murmured, and she realised there was a tear sliding down her cheek. She scrubbed it hastily away.

'Don't be nice to me. I really can't cope with it at the moment. I just need to get through the days.'

'But it's been weeks,' Amy pointed out gently. 'Three weeks? Four?'

'Four weeks and three days. I'm going to move, I think. I told Ben I was, but there haven't been any jobs.'

'You're going to move hospital?' Amy said, her face falling. 'Gosh, I'll miss you.'

'I'll miss you, too, but I can't cope with this. He's just always there, and even when he isn't, I'm looking for him. I'm really sorry, Amy.'

Damn. The tears were welling in earnest now, and she fumbled for a tissue and squeezed her eyes shut.

She could hear Amy moving, shifting her chair, but when she opened her eyes Amy was gone and Ben was there, his eyes tortured.

'What's wrong?' she asked. 'Why are you here?'

'Nothing's wrong. Well, nothing else, apart from you. I can't bear to see you like this, Daisy.'

'Well, hopefully you won't have to for long.

I'm going to start applying for jobs further away. Maybe I'll go back to London.'

'I'll ask Matt if he needs a good registrar.'

'Please don't bother. I don't need to be looking at your doppelganger all day every day.'

He sighed. 'I'll ask around. Maybe there's somewhere else local.'

'You know what? Don't worry. I'll do it myself. It's fine.'

And getting up, she walked away from him, head up, back ramrod straight, and he cursed the day he'd ever set eyes on her and upset the fragile equilibrium of her life.

Cambridge was busy, as bustling as ever, but at least she was away from Ben and Florence, and she found a dress for the wedding.

She needed a smaller size than usual. She was losing weight, because she couldn't summon up the energy or enthusiasm to eat.

'That's fabulous,' Amy said firmly. 'Buy it, and let's go and get lunch. I'm starving.'

Maybe it was the fact that Ben wasn't around, but suddenly Daisy felt—well, not starving, exactly, but certainly hungrier than she had for a while.

Maybe I'm getting over him, she thought hopefully, and then they turned a corner and there was a man ahead of them who, for a fleeting second, looked like Ben, and her heart crashed into her mouth.

Over him? Not in this lifetime.

She drove them back, dropped Amy off and went straight home. Her feet hurt—funny, she was on her feet all day, and yet shopping made her feet hurt like nothing else—and she wanted to shut her front door behind her, kick off her shoes, pull on her sweats and curl up in the corner of the sofa with a cup of tea and the door shut, so she didn't have to listen to Ben and Florence.

But Ben was there, sitting on his doorstep, deep in thought.

Or was he? She opened her mouth, shut it and stood stock still as he got to his feet.

'You must be Daisy,' he said in Ben's voice, and she felt her heart start again.

'Matt?'

He smiled Ben's smile, the smile she hadn't seen for weeks, and held out his hand. 'It's good to meet you—especially since my brother seems to be out. I don't suppose you've got a key?'

'No.' Not any more. And she couldn't leave him standing on the doorstep. 'Why don't you come in?' she offered reluctantly. 'I'm just about to put the kettle on. Is he expecting you?'

'Sort of. I said I'd ring when I got here, but I couldn't give him a time. I've been at work all day.'

'Twins again?'

'No, just paperwork. I gather you've got MCMA twins. That's why I'm here, to see them in the clinic on Monday. I thought, since things were quietish at work, I'd skive off.'

She'd have to warn Amy, she thought. Send her a text, tell her to steer clear. She opened her door, and he stepped over the little fence and followed her in.

How odd. They were almost exactly the same to look at, she thought, eyeing him as he settled at her table and made himself comfortable, and yet there wasn't that tension there that she felt with Ben.

Just what Amy had said, in reverse.

She sent her a text while the kettle was boiling and then reached for the mugs.

'Tea or coffee?'

'Coffee, if there's a choice.'

'Real or instant, caf or decaf?'

He laughed. 'Whatever. Black, one sugar.'

Just like Ben.

She made a pot of real coffee, and sat down at right angles to him at the end. 'Are you hungry? I've got some biscuits.'

'Yes, Florence has told me about your biscuits.'

Did something happen to her face? Because he leant forwards slightly, propping his elbows on the table, and turned his head towards her, his eyes searching hers as she sat down again and slid the biscuits towards him.

'Ben hasn't told me what's happened, but he's stopped talking about you, so I can only imagine it's not going well,' he said quietly. 'Tell me to butt out, but he sounds unhappy.'

She swallowed. Tell him to butt out? How tempting.

'There are reasons,' she said instead.

'There always are.'

'I've warned Amy you're here,' she said, watching him carefully, and he went very still.

'OK. I won't pry if you don't.'

'Deal.'

'He told me you kiss like a goddess, by the way,' he said casually, and she nearly dropped her coffee. So much for the deal!

'When did he tell you that?' she squeaked.

'The day after he met you. Which is unlike him. He's usually much more circumspect.'

'Aren't we all?' she muttered, wondering when Ben was going to get back and take his brother away. 'Why don't you send him a text—tell him you're here?'

'No. He'll be here in ten seconds if I do that, and I'm actually quite happy getting to know the woman who seems to have broken my brother's heart.'

She swallowed. 'What makes you say that?'

He just laughed, as if she'd said something hilarious, and she sighed. 'OK, you can read his mind.'

'I don't have to. He just shuts down. It's easily recognisable.'

'Because you do it?' she asked, and he gave a wry little smile. Funny, she could read him just like she could Ben. The same slight facial movement, the same almost indiscernible shift in expression, and she knew what he was thinking.

'It's a shame, you know. I think he really loves you.'

'I know, but we have reasons.'

'Back to that again,' he said with a faint sigh, and then looked around. 'Nice house. I can see what he saw in his now.'

'I'm moving,' she said, and his eyebrows twitched together.

'Because of Ben?'

Because of Ben, because of Florence. Because her heart couldn't cope with being shredded all over again, a year or so down the line when he'd decided he couldn't handle their relationship after all.

'He says he's good at everything except relationships.'

'False modesty. He's actually very good at relationships. Jane was a one-off, and he never should have married her, but I wasn't much use to him when they started going out.'

She wanted to ask more, but she heard a key in his lock, and the door open and close, then

Florence's little voice saying, 'Can we go and see Daisy, Daddy?'

She bit her lip and turned away, but not before he'd seen the anguish on her face, and with a soft sigh he got to his feet, pressed his hand on her shoulder and thanked her for the coffee.

'Stay there, I'll let myself out,' he said gently, and then he was gone.

She rang Amy.

'Where is he?' she asked, and Daisy could hear the fear in her voice. Fear? Dread?

'He's just gone round to Ben's. He was out, so Matt came and had coffee with me while he waited for him to get back.'

'Um—did he seem OK?'

Except that he'd promised not to pry if Daisy didn't. So no, not really.

'He seemed fine,' she lied. 'He's come up to see the MCMA twins' parents at the clinic on Monday.' And meet the woman who'd broken his brother's heart. As if it wasn't mutual…

'Pity about Daisy.'

Ben froze, the kettle suspended, and shot his brother a killing glance.

'Don't go there.'

'I did. She gave me coffee. She's a lovely woman.'

'Yes—and one day, she'll make someone a wonderful wife.'

'You think?'

'I'm trying *not* to think about her, and you're not helping,' he growled, putting the kettle on to boil. 'So, are you going to see Amy while you're here?' he asked, and turned just in time to see the pain flash in his brother's eyes.

'I don't think that would be a good idea. Daisy's warned her I'm here, anyway, so I imagine she'll make herself scarce. She usually avoids confrontation.'

'Do you want to confront her?'

'Not especially. Look, can we leave this? Some things are just too deep, Ben. Even for us.'

He looked at Matt, at the lines sorrow had carved in his face, and with a rough sigh he turned away, propping his hands on the worktop and staring blindly down the garden.

'I love her,' he said softly, his voice clogged. 'I can't get over her. I fell in love with this house, and then I found her there next door, sexy and funny and kind—so kind, Matt. She's the kindest girl I've ever met. And the sexiest.'

He sucked in a breath, then went on, 'It was all working so well, and being next to her was just perfect. Too perfect, maybe. It was all I could handle, all either of us was ready for, and it was going so well, but then we fell in love and now we've got too much to cope with, too much love, too much emotion. We were burning ourselves out with emotion.'

'And you don't do emotion.'

He raised an eyebrow.

'OK, *we* don't do emotion,' Matt amended.

'I need her in my life, Matt. I can't have her, I can't deal with it, but I sure as hell can't cope without it. Without her.'

Matt propped himself up beside him and stared down the garden with him. 'You are ready to move on, you know. I know you denied it, but you've really fallen for her hard, and she has for you, judging by the look on her face when you and Florence came in. So how are you going to get her back?'

'I can't. She has issues about being a step-mother. She's almost been one, but he was a bastard and the relationship's scarred her, so it's all a bit déjà vu for her, and for me, too. I think she's afraid to trust her heart to anyone else, especially anyone else in the same situation, and I can understand that. Maybe if I'd been single, unencumbered, it might have been different.'

'So she was looking for a clean slate, and she found you?'

'Something like that.'

'So is Florence the stumbling block?'

'Not really. She adores Florence. It's the similarities, for both of us. It plays on our insecurities. I'm another single father with an ex-wife in the background, like the man who broke her heart, and she's on the rebound.'

'Just like Jane.'

'Pretty much. Except Peter's a decent man, unlike Daisy's Mike. And you're right, I am ready to love again. I didn't think I was, but I am, and it was only when she bottled out that I realised how much. But as I say, she's not ready.'

'Could you wait for her?'

He gave a gruff laugh. 'There's no danger I'll be looking around for anyone else, Matt. I've never felt like this before, certainly not with Jane.

She's seeing Peter again, by the way. It's looking serious.'

'Ah. Is he still in the army?'

'Yup. He's coming out in three months, and she's hoping they'll get married. It's what she's always wanted, anyway. What she should have had in the first place.'

Matt gave a quiet sigh. 'And you really don't think there's any hope for you and Daisy?'

'No, because she won't have me. She's told me that, in black and white. Look, can we drop this?'

For a moment Matt said nothing, then he levered himself away from the worktop and frowned at the hob.

'Are you doing anything with that kettle, apart from filling the kitchen with steam?'

'What do you suggest?'

'How about ordering in a curry?'

'I was going to make one.'

'Got beer?'

'Of course.'

'Done. You make the curry, I'll grab a shower, and then we can talk over these twins.'

* * *

She didn't see Matt again.

He and Ben dealt with the Grieves case, and she dealt with the others, and by the time she'd finished, he'd left for London.

It was a pity, she thought, that he hadn't taken his brother with him, but she gritted her teeth and they got through the week, and then it was Laura's wedding—just to rub salt into the wound.

She droved to Nottingham with Amy, and despite her reservations, she had a good time. It would have been better if she'd been happier, but it was good to see the old crowd again and good for her morale to have to fend off the single men. And some who weren't.

They left the next morning after a long breakfast with everyone in the wedding party, and she dropped Amy off and went home, glad it was over. Maybe she could have a bit of peace from weddings now for a while.

As she put her car away, she realised that Ben's car wasn't there, and felt a twinge of disappointment.

Silly. So very, very silly. The sooner she moved, the better.

She let herself in and found her phone blinking,

and scrolled through the call log. Ben had rung her and left a message. So why not her mobile? Because it was still switched off since the wedding, she realised, and stared at the blinking light. For a moment she nearly didn't pick the message up, but then she weakened. It would be something about work, she was sure of it—the MCMA twins, perhaps?

It wasn't.

'Daisy, can you call me as soon as you get this? I'm at the hospital with Florence.'

Oh, dear God. Whatever had happened? Her fingers trembling, she rang him without questioning it. She'd told him to call her if he ever needed her again, and he hadn't. Until now. And if he needed her, for whatever reason, she'd be there for him.

CHAPTER TEN

BEN paced the tiny room, his nerves on edge.

Jane had called him at five thirty that morning, to tell him she felt dreadful. Another migraine, he'd thought dismissively. It wasn't a migraine. It was something much worse, something frightening and potentially threatening to Florence and the status quo.

She was lying in the dark when he got there, and when he went in she moaned and flinched away from the landing light.

'Are you OK?' he asked, instantly concerned.

'No, I feel so ill. I think my head's going to explode,' she whispered. 'Ben, it's never felt like this. I'm scared.'

He didn't mess about. It could have been nothing, or it could have been something very sinister—a bleed, a tumour—or meningitis. Fear clawed at him. What if Florence hadn't just been tired yesterday? She'd been grizzly, fretful, and he'd pretty much dismissed it. But what if…?

He called an ambulance. Then he called Jane's mother, but she was away on holiday, he remembered as the phone rang and rang and rang, and he had no idea how to get hold of Peter. He might even be on a posting abroad, or on some operational exercise.

He found her handbag, her phone and her house keys, threw some basic essentials into a bag and went to let the paramedics in.

Jane was admitted to MAU, and they sent him with Florence to the Paediatric Admissions Unit to be on the safe side. She had bloods taken and all manner of tests and examinations, and now he was waiting for the results, his nerves stretched taut.

And he needed Daisy as he'd never needed her before.

He called her, but her mobile was off, so he left a message on her house phone. Please get it, he thought desperately. Don't go back to Amy's and stay there till the evening. Please go home and find the message and ring me.

She didn't ring, and he tried again. No reply.

He didn't have Amy's number. He could have pulled rank and got it from HR, but it wasn't really necessary, and the only reason he wanted Daisy was for moral support. Well, he'd just have to tough it out.

His ringtone—the one he'd reserved for her—shattered the fraught silence, and he grabbed the phone from his pocket and stabbed the answer button. 'Daisy—thank God,' he said, weak with relief.

'Ben, what's going on? What's happened to her?'

He stepped out of the door so he didn't wake his daughter. 'It's Jane. She's been admitted. She might have meningitis. They're checking Florence to make sure she's OK, but she's been grizzly, and...'

'Do you want me to come?' she asked without hesitation, and he felt his eyes burn. Always thoughtful. Always putting others first. God, he loved her so much.

'If you don't mind.'

'Of course I don't,' she said, and he told her to come to the PAU. Florence was in a vacant side room, just as a precaution, and would stay there until they knew the outcome of both Jane's and her investigations. And now, after a few hours of it, he was tearing his hair out.

Till Daisy walked in and wrapped her arms around him and hugged him hard. He hugged her back, hanging on for dear life, and after a moment she lifted her head and stared up at him, concern transparent in her eyes.

'Any news?'

He shook his head. 'No. They're waiting for the results of Jane's lumbar puncture. If it's bacterial meningitis, then Florence could still be at risk, but they can't find anything wrong with her at the moment except what's most likely a slight cold, so we're probably going to be sent home to watch and wait. I need to distract her because she's worried about Jane and keeps asking for her, but I'm going crazy. I daren't take my eyes off her till I know what it is.'

'What can I do, Ben? Tell me what to do, what you need,' Daisy offered instantly, to his amazement.

He couldn't ask it of her. She'd found the last few weeks incredibly difficult, and he was still feeling guilty—always would—but Daisy assured him it was fine, and he had to believe her because he'd never needed her as he did then.

He wasn't convinced, but he had little choice. 'I need to try and get hold of Peter for her. I'm not sure where he is, but his number's bound to be in her phone and she's got it with her. I ought to check on her, too, see if I can find anything out while I'm there.'

'So go,' she said.

Jane was awake, dazed with pain but coherent enough to speak, and she was desperate to see Peter. 'His number's in my phone,' she said, her voice slurred, and he rang him and filled him in.

'Can I talk to her?' he asked.

'Sure.'

He handed the phone over, and Jane started to cry. He looked away. She loved him, that much was obvious, and from the sound of his voice, Peter loved her, too. He wondered what the future held for them, because it would have a knock-on effect on Florence, and he might end up picking up the pieces.

Suddenly weary, he took the phone back from her when she held it out, and gave Peter directions in the hospital to find the ward.

'He's coming now,' Jane whispered. 'You need to get back to Florence. Who's with her?'

'Daisy,' he said, and she closed her eyes and sighed.

'That's good. Florence loves her—but I thought—'

'Yeah, well, she offered.' Ages ago, but today he'd needed to take her up on it, and she'd come, without a murmur.

He so, so didn't deserve her.

And he wanted her so much.

'Go back to her,' Jane murmured. 'I'll be all right. He'll be here soon.'

He squeezed her hand and left her, hurrying back to the PAU to find Daisy sitting in the chair with Florence on her lap, looking at a book.

'Daddy, Daisy's reading to me!' she announced when he went in, and she sounded much, much better.

'Freddie Frog?' he said with a smile, and Daisy shrugged and smiled.

'It was here.'

'I know. Thank goodness I had the foresight to bring it. It's the only book she likes now.'

Her smile was apologetic. 'I'm sorry.'

'Don't be,' he said. The book was the biggest success story of the year, as far as he was concerned, and he often found her showing the pictures to Froggy in the garden, sitting on the lawn in the shade of the little apple tree and telling him the story.

She'd asked him once if he thought Froggy missed Daisy, and he'd somehow managed to answer her coherently.

Froggy? No. As for Ben himself, that was a different matter, and Florence, too. They both missed her, and the hole in their lives was huge.

They got the all clear to take her home under strict observation, and they went back in convoy. He took Florence inside and got her a drink and a biscuit, and Daisy joined them a few minutes later in the garden.

'I thought you might need some moral support,' she said softly, and settled down cross-legged on the grass next to Florence. She snuggled up to Daisy, her head on her lap and her thumb in her mouth, while Daisy ran her fingers gently through her hair and told her a story.

To look at her, you'd never know there was anything wrong, he thought, staring longingly at

Daisy, that under that serenely smiling exterior her heart was in turmoil, but he knew it must be, because his was, too.

When the story was finished, she helped him with the weeding, and Florence kissed Froggy and hid him for Ben to find, and then ran giggling behind Daisy and hid herself from him, too, and Daisy played along with it like a trouper while Tabitha watched them over the fence from the safety of the conservatory roof.

Florence tried to coax her, but Tabitha just settled down, folded her paws under her chest and watched them play, and Ben, out of the corner of his eye, watched them all and wished that it was real, and all the time the fear was eating at him.

And then the hospital rang him.

He took the call in the kitchen, watching Florence out of the window, feeling as if his whole life was hanging in the balance as he waited for the verdict.

It wasn't bacterial meningitis, it was viral meningitis. Not transmissible in that form, all Florence would get was a cold, if that. Probably the one she had, the little niggle that had made her crabby yesterday and sleepy today.

The relief nearly took the legs out from under him, and he felt his eyes prickle with tears. God, she was so precious to him, so incredibly precious.

'Are you OK?'

He nodded, ended the call and hugged Daisy hard. 'It's viral,' he mumbled into her hair. 'She's fine. They ruled it out with the lumbar puncture, and she's staying in hospital on IV opiates for the pain, and they're going to do scans and blood tests and numerous other things just to be sure, but it's definitely not bacterial meningitis, so Florence is safe. She's just got a little cold.'

'Thank goodness for that,' she said, her voice relieved, and he hugged her again for caring, and for her support, and just because holding her felt so damn good he couldn't let her go.

She eased away. 'So what happens now?'

'God knows. I'll have to wing it. Will you and Evan be able to manage the antenatal clinic without me? And the Grieves twins' check-up? I'm not sure what time their appointment is, I might be able to make it,' he added, thinking on his feet.

'I'm sure we'll cope,' she said calmly. 'I can

email the scans to Matt, can't I, and get his verdict, if necessary. The clinic will be fine.'

'It's not just Monday, Daisy,' he said, troubled. 'I'm on call all week, and Jane's mother's away till Tuesday and in any case she can't do the nights because she takes sleeping pills. It could go on for weeks. What the hell am I going to do?'

'Accept my help?' she said simply, although there was nothing simple about it and they both knew it, but there was no choice for her, Daisy realised. She'd just have to protect her heart as well as she could, but she couldn't walk away from them when they needed her. 'I'll stay with you and cover you when I'm not on call myself. We'll get through this.'

He wanted to hug her again, but it didn't somehow seem like a good idea, so he just thanked her, sighed with relief and went back out to the garden to Florence. She was sitting on the edge of the path talking very seriously to Froggy, and he stood and watched her for a moment, overwhelmed by his love for her.

'She's going to be fine,' Daisy said softly from his side, and he nodded.

She was. But how about them? Daisy was going

to be staying here, in his house, so near and yet so far. How on earth were they going to cope with that?

Jane came out of hospital on Tuesday afternoon, at which point his life went back to normal. Well, his work life, anyway. His home life was a different matter.

Florence stayed with him as planned, and he dropped her off every morning at nursery and picked her up from Jane's when he finished work. Jane wasn't well enough to cope with Florence after nursery school, her head still aching constantly, so her mother did the afternoon nursery school runs and fed her, but she couldn't really cope with much more.

And then there were the nights, and because he was on call for the week, and because nobody was able to swap, it was Daisy who picked up the pieces.

Dear, beloved Daisy, who kept out of the way in her own house all evening unless he had to call on her, and then slept on the sofabed in his sitting room from midnight to six and was gone before Florence woke.

He had to call her back on Thursday morning,

because he was paged by the hospital, and she came round with her hair wound up in a towel and her dressing gown on.

'I don't know if I'll be back in time to take her to nursery,' he said apologetically. 'I could be a while in Theatre, by the sound of it. Nasty RTA. I don't know what I might have to do.'

'Don't worry, I'll take her to nursery, I know where it is.'

'Thanks. I owe you. I'll put the car seat by your car.'

And without thinking, he leant over and kissed her. Just lightly, but it was enough to shock her immobile. Him, too. Their eyes locked, and after a breathless second he moved away, grabbed his keys and went out of the back door.

She sucked in a breath and went upstairs to wake Florence and take her back to her house, armed with her clothes and toothbrush, her lips still tingling.

'Shall we have breakfast?' she asked when they got there, and Florence nodded. They looked in the cupboard and found some cereal, but it was a bit ancient. Daisy tasted it and pulled a face.

'Is it horrid?' Florence asked.

'Very horrid. It's like yucky cardboard. Shall we have toast, instead?'

'I like toast.'

'Good. So do I.'

'Have you got peanut butter? I love peanut butter.'

'No. I've got chocolate spread, though.'

Florence's eyes widened, and Daisy spread it liberally on her toast and then winced as Florence managed to get it all over the table and her face and hands.

While Tabitha licked the table clean, Daisy cleaned her up, swiping the wriggling, giggling child with a damp flannel, and then she took her upstairs to dress them both, wondering as she did so how Ben was getting on.

'I don't want to go to nursery,' Florence told her as they pulled up outside, her bottom lip sticking out. 'I want to stay with you.'

She'd been expecting it. One of the life-skills she'd acquired during her time with Mike had been taking the children to school on occasions, and they'd always tried it on.

'It would be nice, wouldn't it?' she said placidly. 'But I have to go to work and help all the mummies have their new babies, and you have to go to nursery and see all your friends. I tell you what, though, it'll soon be the weekend, and if Daddy has to go to the hospital, if you're a good girl now I'll take you to the playground, and maybe we can take a picnic. How about that?'

She brightened instantly. 'A picnic? Can we take Froggy?'

She stifled a laugh. That wretched concrete frog was destined to feature in every conversation!

'I expect so. Go on, in you go, darling. I'll see you later.'

Florence took two steps up the path, then ran back and reached up, and Daisy bent and kissed her goodbye, her heart contracting as Florence cuddled close for a second before running off again.

Dear, sweet child. She loved her so much. If only she could dare to trust in this love, could trust herself not to fail, could trust Ben not to leave—so many if onlys.

She got back in the car and hurried to work, to find Ben just coming out of Theatre.

'How is she?'

He shook his head. 'Rough, but we saved the baby—thirty seven weeks, perfect little boy and he's doing well. But Mum's got a nasty tear in her liver and massive blood loss. They're working on her now but I don't know if she'll make it, and Dad's got a fractured femur.'

'Oh, Ben, I'm so sorry.'

'Yeah. Life sucks sometimes. I'm just going to find him and tell him he's a father. I'll leave the rest of the news till after he's had his leg pinned. They might know more by then. How's Florence?'

'Fine. She's at nursery, but I had to bribe her with the offer of a picnic in the playground at the weekend.'

He gave a soft huff of laughter, and unexpectedly, his eyes glazed. 'You're such a star,' he murmured, and then dragging in a breath, he walked away to find the father.

She didn't envy him but she knew he'd handle it well, because for all he managed to keep his emotions to himself most of the time, he was very sensitive to other people's feelings.

It was one of the very, very many things about him that she loved.

They met up for coffee, and he was looking happier. 'Sheena Lewis made it,' he told her.

'Your mum with the liver?'

'Yeah. Baby's fine, she's going to recover, Dad's been pinned and plated and the grandparents are on their way to look after the kids. They've got five, apparently—four of his, and this one. They've only been married just under a year.'

'And she's taken on his four children?'

'Mmm. She must be a saint.'

'Or very brave,' she said softly, wishing...

She met the mother later that day, resting quietly in a side room with her baby beside her looking none the worse for wear, and while she was checking Sheena, her mother-in-law came in with two of the children.

'Hello, darlings,' Sheena said weakly, her eyes filling with tears, and they leant carefully over and kissed her cheeks, one each side, their little faces worried.

Bless their little hearts, Daisy thought, and was on her way out when their grandmother stopped her with a gentle hand on her arm.

'Are you attached to her doctor? Ben something, I think?' she asked quietly, and Daisy nodded.

Attached? You could say that, she thought, and resisted the urge to laugh hysterically or burst into tears.

'Yes, I'm his registrar. If you want to talk to him I'm sure he's around.'

'Oh, no, don't disturb him. I just wanted to thank him for saving the baby, and keeping Dan so well informed. He was so worried, and he kept him right up to date apparently and really put his mind at rest. And he didn't lie about how serious it was. Dan was really grateful for that—it meant he could trust him.'

How like Ben. Tell the awful truth, but do it so carefully, so sensitively that it didn't break the person receiving it.

'I'll tell him. Thank you. Please don't make her too tired, will you? She's been through an awful lot.'

'No, we won't, but the children were desperate to see her. My husband's got the younger ones downstairs in the café keeping them amused for a minute, and then we're taking them home.'

'Well, good luck with it. I don't envy you.' *Liar*!

'Oh, we love it, and we'd do anything for them,' Mrs Lewis said with a doting smile.

'Sheena's been a godsend to the family. We all love her to bits.'

'I'm sure you do.'

Daisy summoned a smile and left. If only Mike's family had felt like that. If only *he* had felt like that, instead of just making use of her until he'd convinced his wife to have him back.

No! Stop thinking about the past. It's done. Forget it.

And move on?

She felt a shiver of something. Fear? Anticipation?

Hope?

If only…

Their arrangement worked fine until the weekend, and then all hell broke loose at work and it all got much more complicated.

He was in and out all Friday night, and then again in the morning, and it became obvious to Daisy that she was going to have to be there all the time. And that brought guilt, because Tabitha was getting lonely.

But maybe she didn't need to feel guilty, because Tabitha was also getting braver, and while Daisy was in the kitchen making a picnic to take to the playground, she looked up and found Florence sitting on the lawn with Froggy on one side and Tabitha, just out of reach, on the other, as if she was trying to decide if Florence was OK or not.

She smiled, but it was bitter-sweet. There was no point in Tabitha getting used to Florence, because they were going to move. At least, that was the plan, but she'd done nothing about it. There weren't any jobs, or none that she wanted, and she wasn't going to move until she found one. That would be foolish.

Only marginally less foolish than being here like this with Florence.

Her phone rang, and she glanced at the display as she answered it. 'Hi, Ben. How's it going?'

'OK. Where are you?'

'In the kitchen, making a picnic. Why?'

'Because I'm done here. Are you about to go?

'Yes—five minutes?'

'Make me a sandwich. I'll be with you.'

She slid the phone back in her pocket and sighed. He was hijacking their picnic, taking it and making it something it wasn't meant to be, and she felt sweat break out on her palms.

She could do covering Florence, because that was babysitting in an emergency. But—picnicking with her and her father, in the playground? That was lunacy. Playing happy families, for heavens' sake. Not wise. So, so not wise.

She shut her eyes briefly, then opened them again and reached for the bread, and as she did so, she saw Tabitha curl up beside Florence and settle down, the little girl's hand stroking her incredibly gently, and without warning hot, scalding tears spilled down her cheeks.

He got back just as Daisy put the last few things into a bag.

'Perfect timing,' she said crisply. 'You can carry the lunch. Or Froggy. Take your pick.'

He felt his eyebrows crunch together. 'Froggy?' he said incredulously, and then started to laugh. 'Oh, God, Daisy, we've made a monster.'

'*We* haven't made anything,' she said flatly, and hoisting the bag off the worktop, she went out into the garden, leaving him to follow in confusion.

'Is it time? Are we going?' Florence asked, dancing from foot to foot, and they set off three abreast with Florence skipping in between them.

'Can we do "One two three whee?"' she asked, holding up her arms, and in unison they both said, 'No!'

Their eyes met over her head, remembering her elbow, remembering the conversation they'd had shortly before, in the very playground they were going to. Daisy's eyes clouded, but he was the first to look away.

'We have to be careful with your elbow. You can go on the swing,' he told her firmly.

'Will you push me *really* high?'

'*Really* high,' he promised.

'Can Froggy come on the swing?'

And to think that last week she'd been so subdued, and he'd been worried! Whatever had been wrong with her had clearly passed and left her full of beans, and he wondered what kind of a day Daisy had had with her. Hellish, probably, judging by her rather short greeting.

Oh, damn. Was she mad with him because he'd gatecrashed their picnic? He'd thought it would help, dilute her interaction with Florence, but maybe he'd been wrong. Maybe it just made it worse.

He took Florence on the swing with Froggy

watching safely from the sidelines, and he watched Daisy setting out the picnic out of the corner of his eye. She was kneeling on a rug under a tree, unloading all the goodies, and then she looked up and waved them over.

'Is it time for our picnic?' Florence asked, and she nodded, so Ben lifted her out of the seat and she ran over, settling down cross legged on the rug and patting the space next to her for Froggy—which left a space for him beside Daisy.

Damn. He'd hoped—what had he hoped? That a concrete frog would be enough to keep them apart? Hardly. A brick wall would be more like it. And this had been his idea. He could just as easily have stayed at the hospital, but it didn't seem fair, and after the week they'd all had, he'd just longed to do something normal.

Something a family would do.

He picked up a sandwich at random and bit into it, then stopped in his tracks, his mouth rebelling.

'What…?'

'Chocolate spread,' Daisy said. 'Florence chose it.'

He looked at it in a mixture of confusion and

disgust, and she took pity on him. 'I suppose you'd rather have ham and cheese and chutney?' she said, trying not to laugh, and he handed Florence the chocolate spread sandwich, swallowed the single bite reluctantly and took the sandwich Daisy was offering him.

'Thank you,' he said fervently. 'For a moment there, I thought I was going to have to eat it or starve.'

'Would I do that to you?' she murmured, but he just grunted and ate his sandwich, and she watched Florence chomping her way through the chocolate spread sandwich and a small banana and some crisps, in no particular order, and wished she could bottle this moment and get it out, in the long dark days ahead after she'd found another job and moved away and Florence and Ben were in the past.

She picked a daisy out of the grass, and then another, absently slitting the stem of the first and threading the other through it, then adding another, and another—

'What are you doing?' Florence asked curiously, and she blinked and dragged herself back to the here and now.

'Making a daisy chain. It doesn't matter if we pick them, the daisies are weeds, really, they don't belong here.' Funny, that, she thought. Another Daisy that didn't belong. 'Look—if you slit the stem with your nail, and you're very careful, you can thread another one through, and if you do it enough times you can make a necklace.'

Florence's little fingers couldn't manage, but she could pick them, very carefully. 'Keep the stems as long as you can,' Daisy asked, 'and mind you don't squash them.'

And as Ben watched and Florence brought her the little white flowers that didn't belong, she made a necklace for Florence and put it over her head. 'There you go, Princess. Your very own daisy chain.'

Her eyes were huge blue saucers. 'It's *really* pretty,' she said, stroking it as carefully as she would a tiny bird. 'Daddy, look!'

'I'm looking,' he said gruffly, and Daisy glanced up and caught his eyes, and her breath jammed in her throat.

Oh, no. No, no, no! They weren't supposed to be doing this! Where was his pager when she needed it? Not that she wanted some poor woman to have an emergency, but if anybody was planning one, now would be a good time.

Nobody was.

And Ben, lounging back on one elbow so he was half facing her, plucked a daisy off the little pile that Florence had created and fingered it thoughtfully.

'I can remember, when we were kids, the girls would get a daisy and pull the petals off, one by one, and as they did it they'd say, "He loves me," then "he loves me not," each time they'd pull a petal out, like this, until they got to the last one, and then they'd pull it out, too, like this—"He loves me",' he ended, pulling the last few petals out in one and looking straight into Daisy's eyes.

He loves me.

She swallowed and looked hastily away.

'What does he loves me not mean?' Florence asked.

'It means he doesn't love me,' Daisy told her, and looked pointedly at Ben, who just smiled sadly and got to his feet.

'Come on, Florence. Let's go on the see-saw.'

'With Daisy!' she squealed, getting to her feet

and pulling Daisy up, and what was she supposed to say to that?

Staring daggers at him, she sat on the end of the see-saw, Florence cuddled up to her as she'd been before, all those weeks ago, and damn him, he just smiled sadly at her and rocked them gently up and down, up and down, singing, 'See-saw, Marjorie Daw, Johnny shall have a new master,' his deep voice soft and warm and curiously comforting. Daisy closed her eyes so she didn't have to look at him, but she could still hear him, could imagine him quietly rocking a baby and singing nursery rhymes, and her heart was splintering as he sang, and the see-saw rose and fell, and rose and fell, until at last she couldn't bear it any more.

'I want to get off,' she said firmly, and he stopped, so her feet were just off the ground and their eyes were locked.

'Count the petals on a daisy, Daisy,' he said softly, and let her down.

She got off. 'They have an even number,' she said expressionlessly, and walked away.

He watched her packing up the picnic, and with a quiet sigh he got off the see-saw and took Florence to play on the slide. He didn't know what to do. He loved her. She loved him, and she loved Florence. If only she could believe in them, then maybe he could dare to hope…

CHAPTER ELEVEN

His pager went off just as Florence was settled in her bed.

Daisy had gone home as soon as they'd got back from their picnic. 'Call me if you need me,' she'd said, and walked out, leaving Florence confused and disappointed, because she'd wanted Daisy to read her a story. Even Tabitha, sunning herself in the garden, had looked confused when she disappeared.

And it was his fault, apparently. Well, that didn't surprise him. The atmosphere between them had been fraught since the moment he'd come home from the hospital, and apart from a brief interlude in the playground, it hadn't improved since.

So she'd gone home—to regroup, presumably, and rant about him in private—and he'd put Florence to bed. He'd really hoped he wouldn't need her, so that she could have some time away from the situation to chill out and destress, but the pager wasn't on their side.

He was reaching for the phone to call her when she knocked on the door and walked in. 'I heard the pager,' she said flatly. 'I hope you aren't going to be long, I wanted a bath tonight.'

'Have one here. I could be ages, judging by the look of this. It's a breech that's on a go-slow, so fill the bath and take your time. There's wine in the fridge and Florence is in bed.'

Wine. That was all she needed, on an empty stomach. But the bath? Oh, yes. She went back to her house, grabbed her things—bubble bath, her razor, deodorant, moisturiser, body butter—she was really going to go for it, and if he was back in ten minutes, tough, because she wasn't in the mood to hurry. At all.

She ran the bath, thought why not, went and got a glass of wine and slid under the bubbles. Bliss. There were no candles—maybe not a good idea with a child in the house, but a luxury she longed for. She glanced mournfully at the wall, picturing her bathroom on the other side of it, her sanctuary.

This room was clean, efficient and masculine,

dominated by a huge walk-in shower, and his things were all over it. His dressing gown on the back of the door, his toothbrush on the basin. A pair of jeans had been chucked in the corner, next to Florence's tiny little pink knickers and a T-shirt with a frog on it.

Oh, damn you, Ben Walker, damn you and your gorgeous little daughter and your 'he loves me, he loves me not' nonsense. She had no idea how many petals there were on a daisy, and she was absolutely *not* counting them!

She sipped the wine, sighed and slid a little lower under the bubbles. Mmm. Better. Half an hour of this, and maybe she'd feel a lot less fraught and a little bit more reasonable.

'Daisy?'

The house was in darkness, except for the nightlight spilling from Florence's room. He put the hall lights on and went up to check, but there was no sign of her, just Tabitha curled up in a ball at the foot of Florence's bed, next to the frog cushion. He ought to move her, he thought, but then he shrugged. He'd had cats on the bed all his childhood and they'd never done him any harm. He pulled the door to, and paused outside the bathroom to listen.

Nothing.

'Daisy?' he murmured, and tapped very lightly so as not to wake Florence, but there was no reply.

Where the hell was she? She was supposed to be looking after Florence, and she'd clearly gone home—and some time ago, because it was dark outside now, and it was three hours since he'd left, so she hadn't just nipped out to fetch something from next door or the lights would still be on.

But there were no lights on in her house, either, and she wouldn't just leave Florence, she wasn't irresponsible. Had she had an accident? Surely she couldn't *still* be in the bath?

He opened the door quietly, and his breath left him in a soft huff of relief, mingled with regret and a deep and painful yearning.

Oh, Daisy.

She was in the bath, her eyes closed, fingers loosely wrapped around a wine glass balanced precariously on her sternum, and through the very few bubbles that still floated on the surface, he could see her chest rising and falling gently, rocking the half-full glass with every breath.

Sleeping Beauty meets the Siren on the Rocks, he thought, and walked up to her, perching on the edge of the bath and staring down at her, mesmerised. God, she was gorgeous. Even like that, with her mouth hanging slightly open and her fingers round a wine glass, looking for all the world like a lush.

He smiled fondly and eased the glass out of her fingers, waking her abruptly. Startled, she sat up, clutching her arms across her chest and staring at him with wild eyes as the water sloshed and settled. Then she let out her breath on a gasp.

'Ben! Gosh, you scared the living daylights out of me. Is Florence all right?'

'She's fine,' he said, stifling a smile. 'Why don't you get out of there and dry off and come downstairs and I'll get you another glass of wine. Have you eaten tonight?'

She shook her head. 'No, not yet. What's the time? The water's freezing.'

'I'm not surprised, it's ten o'clock. I'll call a takeaway. What do you fancy?'

She looked at him, her lips parting slightly, her

eyes unreadable in the soft flood of light from the landing. He thought she might be blushing, and it made him want to smile. Or kiss her.

'Anything. Go away, Ben—and shut the door behind you!' she squeaked, her modesty returning as she woke up properly.

He left her with the tatters of her dignity, changed his trousers because they'd got soaked when she sat up so abruptly, and went downstairs to phone for a takeaway. Even if he had to go out again before it arrived, she could eat, and if she was feeling mellow maybe she'd even save him some.

She came down a few minutes later, wrapped in her dressing gown and looking tousled and delectable. She smelt gorgeous, and he wanted to pull her into his arms and just hold her.

'I'm sorry I've been crabby,' she said, before he could do anything so rash. Just as well. And maybe it would make sense to talk.

'Why have you? Because I gatecrashed your picnic?'

'Partly,' she admitted. 'It took it from me baby-sitting to something else, something we'd agreed we wouldn't do any more. And then when we got there, there was all that silly *nonsense* with the daisies.'

'What silly nonsense was that?' he asked, perfectly serious, and her heart thumped in her chest.

'You were pushing my buttons, Ben.'

'I was telling you that I still love you.'

She felt her eyes fill, and looked hastily away. 'Ben, we can't—'

'Why can't we? I've been thinking about it a lot—endlessly, in fact. About why you're so worried about us. And I don't think it's anything to do with Florence—'

'I don't want to hurt her!'

'But you won't. She adores you, Daisy, and you adore her. And I know you'll never hurt her.'

'But she will be hurt—when we split up, she *will* be hurt.'

'What if we don't?'

She turned slowly and looked at him. 'What are you saying?'

'I'm saying maybe we didn't give ourselves enough time. Maybe we didn't get to know each other well enough. As far as Daisy's concerned, you're just a friend of mine who lives next door and does stuff with us occasionally. If we give ourselves another chance, spend some time alone together, without changing anything with Florence, then maybe we could learn to trust each other. Maybe we could make it work.'

'And if we can't?'

'Then she won't be hurt any more than she is now, and at least we will have tried.'

She felt a tiny stirring of hope, but she didn't dare let it grow. Not just yet.

'What about Jane? What will she think?'

'Don't worry about Jane. I saw her yesterday when I picked Florence up, and Peter arrived while I was there. He's there for the weekend, and he scooped Florence up and gave her a big kiss hello, and she hugged him and called him Uncle Peter. And Jane took me on one side and told me that they're thinking of getting married. And Florence doesn't seem even slightly fazed by him being around.'

'Are you?' she asked, reading his eyes carefully, because Mike would have gone into orbit if his wife had even looked at another man, but Ben just shook his head.

'Why would I be? Except in so far as it affects Florence, and it really doesn't seem to. She clearly likes him, and Jane's been in love with him for years. He wouldn't marry her before because he was in the army bomb disposal team, and he didn't want her ending up a widow. We met at a mutual friend's wedding a few months after they split up, and I think she'd decided then that it was time to move on. And I was there, physically and mentally sound, single, ready for a permanent relationship, and I had decent career prospects. And if she couldn't have Peter, then I ticked all the necessary boxes. And then she forgot to take her pill one day and got pregnant.'

'So you married her.'

'Yes. She was having my child, and to be honest she ticked the boxes for me in the same sort of way. Matt tried to warn me that it wasn't enough, but he had his own problems at the time and I ignored him, because following his heart didn't seem to have done him any good. And after we were married, I realised he was right. Jane was lonely, she wanted to come back here to be near her family, and of course she missed Peter. He's from round here, too, and I think that was a big part of her wanting to come back.'

'Did you know about him?' she asked, appalled

that he might have found out after they were married—or at least, after it was too late.

'I did by then. She'd realised she didn't love me, and she didn't want to be with me. She said it wouldn't be good for Florence anyway to have unhappy parents who were stuck with each other in a relationship that was going nowhere. I didn't agree at the time, I thought she was using me and maybe had all along, but maybe I agree now, now I can see that it works. Anyway, we split up and she moved up here, and as soon as I could get a job in the area, I was to move closer so I could share Florence's care. And in the time it took for that to happen, Peter came back into her life.'

'But I thought he was still in the army?'

'He is, but he's just reaching the end of his commission and he'll be UK based now to the end, but you've only got to see them together to see how well it works for them. I know they'll be all right, and he's a thoroughly decent guy.'

Her heart was thumping. 'So—you're not worried about Florence being upset by you having a relationship with me? If—if we felt it could work? I mean—*really* work.'

He gave a fleeting smile, and grazed her cheek

gently with his knuckles. 'No. Not at all. Not now I know you, because I know you'd never hurt her. Jane says she talks about you all the time and seems very fond of you, and if we don't involve her any more than we already have until we're both utterly sure about it, then I can't see it'll do her any harm. And I can't go on like this, Daisy. I really miss you, and I really want to see if what we've got could work. I'm not on call after tomorrow, and Jane's better now, so Florence will be back there from tomorrow night.'

And they could be alone. It was written in his eyes, in the longing and hope she could read there so clearly, and it echoed the longing she didn't dare give a voice to.

'Please give me a chance,' he went on, his voice serious. 'Let me prove to you that this can work. Give me this coming week—and next weekend. Maybe Jane can have Florence and we can spend some time together doing fun stuff.'

'I might be working.'

'You aren't. I changed the rota.'

She opened her mouth to tell him not to interfere, and then she caught the uncertainty in his eyes.

'OK,' she said, capitulating, but with reservations. 'We'll try. This week. I don't know about the weekend yet.'

'Just don't rule it out.'

He hugged her briefly, but before her arms could come up and circle him and hold him to her heart, the knocker sounded.

'That'll be our food,' he said, and let her go, and she sucked in a deep breath and closed her eyes.

What on *earth* had she just done?

She woke up on Monday morning tingling with anticipation. Ben had been called out again Sunday night and he'd sent her home.

'Tomorrow. I don't want any interruptions,' he'd said, with a promise in his eyes, and she'd gone home to bed alone. It was lovely to sleep in it again, after a week on Ben's sofa bed, and she woke refreshed and looking forward to going to work for the first time since their breakup.

Ever since then she'd been avoiding him, trying to keep out of his way, and when they'd been forced together there'd been a tension that she was sure everyone would have felt.

But now—now it was back to how it had been, working together seamlessly through the ward round and the routine of the morning, then Mel and Adrian Grieves came into the antenatal clinic for their check-up scan on the monoamniotic twins. They were twenty four weeks now, and although there was a loose tangle that didn't seem to want to untangle, both twins were growing well, their heartbeats were strong and healthy, and Ben was happy.

So were the parents.

'Are they viable now?' Mel asked, and Ben pulled a face.

'At a push. I wouldn't want to deliver them yet, not for at least eight more weeks, but they would stand a chance now, yes.'

The tension went out of her, and her husband squeezed her shoulder as her eyes welled with tears. 'I've been so scared for them. It just seems to have been such a long time.'

'Well, it isn't over yet, but we'll have you in in a few more weeks—maybe two? The cords *are* tangled, and I do have a little bit of concern, but at the moment they're fine and I'm happy to leave them. If they get another loop in that tangle, I'll want you here, so maybe from next week have a bag in the car with you, just in case. OK?'

She nodded, looking almost excited, as if for the first time she dared to let herself believe it could be all right.

'Do you think they'll make it?' Daisy asked Ben when they'd left.

'I hope so. I want you in charge of them when she's admitted. Daily scans, Doppler three times a day, at least, and really close scrutiny. If she feels they're moving a lot it could be because there's a problem, so I want her checked again then, day or night.'

He broke off and met her eyes searchingly. 'You will be here, won't you? Until we deliver them? I really want you in charge of the day-to-day running of this case, even if we...'

'Don't you trust Evan?'

'Trust? Yes, of course I do, he's a box-ticker and he wouldn't let anything happen to them, but I don't think he's right for Mel. I want *you*,' he said quietly. 'Mel knows you, and so do I. And you don't have an ego so you won't try to go it alone if you're worried.'

She gave a wry little laugh. 'Fair point. But

there aren't any jobs for me to go to anyway, so even if we decide it doesn't work, you'll be stuck with me for a while, so, yeah, I'll be here.'

His gaze didn't flicker from her eyes. 'Good, because I feel we could be getting somewhere now. Give us time, Daisy. Please. And have a little faith in me.'

She felt her smile slip, and nodded. 'I will. And whatever happens, I'll stay for the twins at least.'

He levered himself off the edge of the desk and took her shoulders in his hands. 'Thank you,' he said quietly, and folded her into his arms for a brief and gentle hug. Then dropping a kiss on her hair, he eased away and swatted her lightly on the bottom. 'Off you go, Dr Daisy, before I do something unprofessional to you halfway through the antenatal clinic. And I'm cooking for you tonight, by the way.'

'I'll look forward to it,' she said, and went off to find her next patient, her heart lighter than it had been for weeks.

He sent her off for a relaxing bath in her lovely sanctuary when she got home from work, and when she came down, the dining room was transformed.

He'd cooked her a meal, laid the table, lit candles—but they didn't get that far. He poured her a glass of wine, handed it to her and kissed her fleetingly, then the wine glass ended up on the table and she ended up in his arms.

'Oh, Daisy, I've missed you so damn much,' he said raggedly into her hair, cradling her close. 'Missed having you to myself, missed spending time alone with you doing nothing in particular, just being with you. And it feels *so* good just to hold you.'

She lifted her head and looked up into his eyes. 'Will supper keep?'

He went over to the hob, drained the potatoes, turned off the heat under the casserole and came back to her. 'It will now,' he said, smiling as he cradled her face in his hands and kissed her lingeringly. 'Did you have anything special in mind?'

They ate later, with the candles burned down and the casserole well and truly tender, and Tabitha mugged him for scraps which he gave her without question.

'You shouldn't feed her at the table,' she said disapprovingly, but in fact she was glad he did, glad he didn't mind the cat, because she was spending more and more time next door, and on Saturday night she'd slept on Florence's bed. And if—

Don't jump the gun! she warned herself, and put another scoop of his delicious casserole on her plate.

'No!' she told the cat and put her on the floor. 'You see what you've done?'

His eyes twinkled. 'Mmm. Turned her into a normal cat. What a shame. Do you want these green beans, or shall I finish them?'

Sheena Lewis was making steady progress after her car accident, and Daisy went in to check her on Tuesday afternoon just as her husband and the children were leaving. He was in a wheel-chair, and the oldest two were squabbling good-naturedly over who was going to push him back to the ward.

'Hey, take it in turns or you won't be allowed to push it, because you'll hurt him,' Sheena said. 'Lucy first, she's oldest. And where's my kiss goodbye?'

The children ran to hug her, not a sign of the

dutiful about them, both of them obviously devoted to their stepmother. She'd seen them before, last Friday, and they looked a great deal happier now that both their parents were on the mend.

'Come on, horrors, let's leave Sheena with the doctor,' Dan Lewis said, and they left. Sheena flopped back against the pillows with a weary smile and sighed with relief, and Daisy chuckled as she turned back the covers and had a look at her wound.

'That's coming on really well. It looks lovely and clean. You should be able to go home soon.'

'Good. I think Dan's parents are finding it all a bit much. Still, he'll be home tomorrow so he can help to keep them in order.'

'They're quite a handful, I imagine,' Daisy said, wondering how she coped, but she just smilingly agreed.

'Oh, they are, but I wouldn't change them for the world. They're the sweetest things, and they lost their mother four years ago, so they've been really upset by this accident. I think they wondered if it might not all happen again, and the fact that we're both all right and the baby's here is just a bit much for them on top of the shock, so they're a bit like a bottle of fizzy drink that's been shaken—open with care! But they're such good kids. Dan was saying earlier that if he'd died, he wouldn't have had to worry about the kids because he would have known they'd be all right.'

'It's a lot to take on. They're lucky to have you,' Daisy said quietly, and she shrugged.

'I fell in love with Dan, and the kids are part of him. How couldn't I love them? It hasn't all been easy, don't think that, but I wouldn't give back a minute of it. It's been wonderful, and it's just got better, and I'm just so grateful that I'm alive to share it.'

'I bet you are,' Daisy said softly, and left her in peace. She told Ben about their conversation later, over dinner, and he winced.

'I didn't realise their mother was dead. Poor little things.'

'Mmm. She said Dan feels he doesn't have to worry about anything happening to him because they'll be all right with her.'

'I can understand that,' he said, surprising her. 'If anything happened to me and Jane wasn't around for any reason, if you were there I'd know Florence would be safe and secure and loved.'

He trusted her that much? Feeling choked, she laid a hand over his and squeezed it. 'Thank you.'

He turned his hand over and caught hers, threading their fingers together. 'What for? It's the truth, Daisy. You love her, and given the slightest encouragement, she'll love you, too. She probably already does. It's not hard, after all.'

'Too hard for Mike.'

'Tell me about him,' he urged softly, and she shrugged.

'Oh—what's to tell? He just messed me about. He kept saying we'd get married one day, maybe, but he just wouldn't set a date. He never really asked me, and he certainly didn't give me a ring. I don't think he had any intention of doing it, he was just looking for someone to help with the kids at weekends, and then he realised how busy I was and how much he was still having to do, so when his wife said she'd have him back, he dropped me like a hot brick—but he'd talked about us getting married in front of the children, so they were really confused because it just didn't happen. Kids are too immediate. If you tell them you're getting married, they want to know when, and they want it to be in the foreseeable future. "Sometime" just isn't good enough, it's like saying "Maybe" when they ask if they can do something. It means no. I should have realised that, pinned him down and forced his hand, and it would have been over earlier.'

'No,' he said flatly. 'He should have been more straightforward with you. And if he wanted to marry you, he should have asked you properly. He was just wasting your time, using you, and I'd quite appreciate a few minutes alone with him.'

He let go of her hand and cleared the table, and they made tea and took it into the sitting room in front of the television and watched the news with Tabitha lying sprawled across them both, Ben's arm around Daisy's shoulders, snuggling her close and making her feel safe and wanted.

Loved.

It was a wonderful feeling. Dare she trust it? She was still afraid of making a mistake, of doing something that could hurt an innocent child as Freya and Millie had been hurt—as she'd been hurt—but there were lots of people who made second marriages work.

Take Sheena Lewis. She was amazing with her stepchildren, and Ben had said he felt the same way about her and Florence as Dan did about Sheena and the children.

He trusted her that much. He trusted her with his beloved child. Could she trust him?

Yes. Surely, yes.

She snuggled closer, and he turned off the television and lifted the cat off onto the floor. 'Bedtime,' he said, a smile flickering in the back of his eyes, and she slipped her hand through his and let him lead her up to bed.

'Jane and Peter can't have Florence this weekend, they're going away,' he told her on Thursday morning, when she'd been looking forward to it for days.

'Oh. Well, it doesn't matter,' she said, surprised at how disappointed she felt, but Ben just smiled and pulled the rabbit out of the hat.

'I've got a better idea. Let's go to Yorkshire and see my parents. We'll have resident babysitters, and it's ages since they've seen her, and I can show you where I grew up.'

He was taking her to meet his parents? Wow.

That was progress. She'd never met Mike's parents—but then, as she'd realised belatedly, he'd never been serious about her, so why would she have done? She'd never been that important.

But she was important to Ben. Very important, and this weekend suddenly took on a whole new meaning of its own.

They were leaving at four on Friday afternoon, straight from work.

'Bring a dress,' he'd said. 'I've booked a table for Saturday night, and it's quite smart.'

'How smart?'

He shrugged. 'I'll wear my suit, since you rescued it for me and it's survived. Probably not a tie.'

The dress she'd had for Laura's wedding? She'd only worn it once, and it was lovely. She felt really good in it, and it was the sort of material that packed well. 'What else?'

'Jeans and walking shoes. And just normal stuff. We'll take my parents and Florence to Bettys for tea.'

'Oh, I've heard of Bettys tearoom! Can we really go?'

'Yes. I've booked that, too.'

'You're a marvel of organisation,' she said with a smile, and packed. Then repacked, because she was taking far too much, and she realised she was nervous.

They set off promptly, leaving Evan in charge with strict instructions to contact Ben if anything happened with the twins, and they arrived at eight, just as the sun was going down.

It was a stone farmhouse, right on the outskirts of Harrogate, with spectacular views over the Yorkshire countryside. She could see the sun setting in the distance as he turned onto the drive, and as he pulled up outside three dogs came running towards them, tails lashing.

'Hello, girls,' he said, getting out of the car and greeting them, and then they rushed round to greet Daisy as Ben lifted Florence out of her seat in the back. 'I'll get the luggage in a minute,' he murmured, Florence's head lolling on his shoulder, and putting his arm round Daisy, he led her into the house, the dogs at their feet.

She felt ridiculously nervous.

Was her hair a mess? Her makeup smudged? She'd probably got cake crumbs round her mouth from snacking in the car—

'You look fine,' he said, his eyes laughing as he pushed the back door open and went in. 'Hi, Mum.'

His mother was lovely. Warm and homely, practical, no-nonsense, with an apron tied firmly round her middle and a kitchen that smelled of heaven. 'You must be Daisy,' she said, beaming. 'I'm Liz.' And without hesitation, she hugged her. 'Andrew's about somewhere—ah, there you are, darling. They're here.'

'Dad, this is Daisy. Daisy, my father Andrew.' Ben kissed his mother's cheek, handed her the sleeping child, hugged his father and put the kettle on.

'If I don't make Daisy a cup of tea soon, she'll kill me,' he said mildly. 'But if you're opening a bottle of wine, Dad, I'm with you all the way.'

'It's done.' He shook her hand firmly. 'Hello, Daisy, it's lovely to meet you.'

'You, too. I've heard a lot about you. Apparently I have "good hands" like you when I'm operating.'

His father chuckled. 'Oh, dear. I hope you weren't too insulted.'

'I told her not to be. Mum, that is seriously

good chilli,' he said, putting the lid back on the pot and licking the spoon. 'I'm starving.'

'You're always starving. I've made plenty.'

'Good. Where have you put us?'

His mother's face was bland. 'I've made up the guest room and your room, and Florence is in the little room. Take your pick. Bring your bags in and you can put her to bed before we eat. She's exhausted, poor little mite. Has she eaten enough?'

'Plenty,' he said, laughing. 'Dad, can you give me a hand?'

'So where *are* we sleeping?' she asked later as they were going up to bed.

'If Florence wasn't here, I'd say my room. As it is, I think I'd better show you to your room and kiss you goodnight.'

Pity. She could have done with a cuddle.

She got one. Too brief, but a very definite cuddle.

'They're lovely,' she mumbled into his shirt.

'They are. They think you are, too.'

He kissed her, then kissed her again, just in case she'd missed it the first time, and she had to push him away laughing.

'Go on, go to bed. What are we doing tomorrow?'

'Breakfast, walking the dogs, light lunch, then afternoon tea in Bettys, and then back here to get ready for dinner. And then after dinner,' he said, his eyes twinkling, 'I might have to introduce you to the hay barn.'

'Gosh, you know how to treat a girl,' she laughed, and pushed him away again. 'Go on, out, before you have any more silly ideas.'

He went.

CHAPTER TWELVE

IT WAS, as he'd said, an action-packed day.

They left Florence feeding the animals with her grandparents and walked for miles over the Yorkshire Dales, the dogs trotting happily alongside them. The weather was glorious—not too hot, and with a light breeze to cool her skin, but he'd smothered her in sun screen just to be on the safe side, and found her a hat.

He swiped it off and sang, 'On Ilkley Moor Bar T'at' to her in his lovely rich, deep voice with a good helping of Yorkshire, making her laugh, and they sat down under an outcrop of rocks to rest for a while. He wrapped his arm round her and hugged her against his side, and she sighed with contentment.

'It's beautiful,' she said, looking out across the moors, and he made a soft sound of agreement.

'I love it here. I often come here, when it's all too much.'

'Is it, often?'

His smile was pensive. 'It has been. It's getting a whole lot better,' he said, and kissed her.

After a very light lunch they went into Harrogate and had the most wonderful afternoon tea at Bettys, served on three-tier silver cake stands, to the sounds of the resident pianist playing softly in the background. Florence was in her element, and she wriggled to the edge of her seat and ate her sandwich, then two tiny fondant fancies, and another sandwich.

'Someone won't want any more tonight,' Andrew said with an indulgent smile, and Ben chuckled.

'You'll be amazed. The child has hollow legs.'

'More than I have,' Daisy said, wondering how she'd get through dinner, but by the time she was dressed and ready, her stomach was churning a little.

With hunger? Or something else?

Florence was downstairs with Ben in the kitchen when she went down there, and there was no sign of the others.

'Will I do?' she asked, and his eyes softened.

'Oh, yes. You'll do,' he said, and smiled down at Florence. 'Shall we sing Daisy that song?'

'What song?' Daisy asked, expecting another silly Yorkshire ditty, but he crouched down, sat Florence on one knee with the other one on the ground to steady himself, and counted Florence in, then started to sing.

'One, two, three, "Daisy, Daisy, give me your answer, please."'

Daisy laughed. 'It's not please.'

'Oh, yes, it is. Hush now, listen. Ready? "I'm half crazy all for the love of these."'

She laughed again. 'It's not—'

He lifted a warning finger, his eyes twinkling, and Florence shushed her. 'It's very hard, don't laugh!' she said seriously.

So Daisy stopped laughing, and listened to them, Ben coaxing Florence along as she stumbled on the words.

'"It won't be a stylish marriage, I can't afford a carriage, but you'll look sweet, upon the seat of a bicycle made for three."'

She stared at him. He was kneeling on one knee, looking up at her intently, and her heart began to pound.

The laughter was gone, his eyes deadly serious. 'Ben?'

'Did you like it?' Florence asked, running up to her and grabbing her hand, her eyes alight. 'Did you like our song?'

'Um—yes, it was lovely, darling.' Utterly charming, and she felt a strange sensation all over her body, a tingling, fizzing sensation, like champagne bubbles bursting through her veins. Was he—?

He was on his feet now, brushing off the knee of his horribly expensive suit and smiling at her. 'Come on, our taxi's here. Off to bed, poppet. Go and find Grannie and tell her we'll see her later. Kiss!'

He bent down and kissed her, and she hugged Daisy and kissed her, too, and then skipped out, humming the tune a little off-key.

'Got a cardigan in case it's cold later?'

'Um—I've brought a wrap,' she said, still slightly stunned and a little off balance.

'Great. Come on, then, let's make a move.'

He seemed oddly tense suddenly, and he was quiet all the way there. He paid the taxi driver, then threaded his fingers through hers as they walked to the restaurant.

'Oh, Ben, it's lovely.'

'Hope so. I've never been.'

They were ushered to a table in an alcove, and the service was incredible. Swift and unobtrusive, and the food was amazing.

'I've chosen the menu—I hope you don't mind,' he said as they sat down, but she just shrugged, a little puzzled but prepared to go along with him, because there was something about him...

They had a starter of fish and chips—a tiny cone, with minute goujons of sole and the sweetest little French fries.

'Gosh—the portions are a bit more delicate than the ones we got the from the Yoxburgh chippy,' she said with a delighted laugh.

His eyes were strangely intense. 'That was the night you told me you love me,' he murmured, and her breath eased out on a sigh.

Oh, Ben. You sentimental thing...

The starter was followed by sea bass.

She looked at it, then at him, and he just smiled. 'I fell in love with you over the sea bass,' he said softly, as if that explained everything, and her heart started to beat a little faster.

She smiled at him, her heart full. 'I think I fell in love with you when I opened the door and saw you covered in soggy plaster. It was the power suit that did it, of course. It looks good on you. I'm glad it survived.'

He laughed softly and topped up her wine.

'Eat up. We've got a special dessert coming.'

'Really? I'm going to struggle.'

'I'm sure you'll cope. It's very light. It's carrot based.'

'Carrot?' She laughed, fascinated, but she ate up as instructed, savouring every mouthful, the butterflies settling down now as he started to talk to her about his childhood.

And then his marriage.

'I think the problem with it was that it wasn't real. We didn't really love each other—there was no deep-rooted connection between us, and I don't think there was between you and Mike. I don't know how you feel, but it's as if I've never really been married—never known before I met you what it is to get to the end of the working day and long to get home to see the person I was sharing my life with. And when it all disintegrated, I wasn't that gutted, really. It didn't seem such a great loss.'

'Oh, Ben, that's so sad,' she said. 'And you're right. I didn't know Mike. I thought I did, I thought I loved him, but I just wanted to, really, and wanted him to love me, so we could make a life together for the girls, but he didn't care about any of us. Not like you.'

'I didn't want to love you. No, I did. I was afraid to,' he said honestly, and signalled to the waiter. Their plates were whisked away, and he reached over and took her hands in his, his eyes curiously intense.

'I'd decided I'd be alone. It was easier that way, less complicated, and it meant I could concentrate on Florence. I never expected to find anyone like you. It's the first time I've ever met anyone I want to spend the rest of my life with, and it's just utterly different. I didn't know what love was until I met you, Daisy, and now I do, well—I don't want to let it go.'

He glanced up and let go of her hands, and a waiter placed a dish in the centre of the table between them. It was covered with a silver dome, and he bowed slightly and lifted it away with a flourish.

It was a pile of ice chips.

Very pretty ice chips—a little heap, decorated with rose petals, the one in the middle sparkling in the candlelight.

She leant over, frowning slightly, not quite sure…

'I thought you said it was carrot based?' she murmured, puzzled.

Ben reached into the pile of ice and drew out the centre one, the one that sparkled. Only it wasn't ice at all, it was—

Carat, she thought, not *carrot*, and her heart did a little skitter.

The waiter removed the dish, and Ben took her hand in his. 'I love you, Daisy Fuller. I think it was the sea bass, but it could have been the tea all down your dressing gown,' he said, making her laugh. Or cry. She wasn't sure. And he was humming now, the tune he'd sung with Florence. Just a few bars, and then he broke off.

'I don't want to go down on one knee in front of everyone, but I will, if it'll make a difference. So what's your answer, Daisy?' he asked softly.

'If I promise to keep the plumbing in order and not complain about chocolate spread sandwiches, will you marry me? Will you be my wife, and give me and Florence all the love I know is in your heart?'

His mouth was smiling, but his eyes were uncertain, and she couldn't let him struggle. 'Yes,' she said softly, tears filling her eyes. 'Oh, yes, Ben, of course I will. I love you—I'll always love you. And I'll love Florence as if she's my own.'

He let his breath out on a shuddering sigh, smiled and slipped the ring onto her finger, then stood up and pulled her up into his arms, laughing and hugging her until she thought her ribs might break. And then he let her go, just a little, and looked down into her eyes and kissed her.

'Time to go somewhere a little more private,' he murmured, and she realised that everyone was clapping and cheering.

Ben let her go. A little. He still kept his arm around her firmly, but he smiled down at her, his eyes glowing.

'I want to set a date. And I want it to be soon.'
'For Florence?'

'For all of us, because until we're married, we can't be together when she's there, and I'm an impatient man, I've realised. So—how quickly can we organise a wedding?'

She smiled. 'Very quickly. I have two experts lined up who've just done it. I'll pick their brains.'

'Good.' He topped up her champagne and held the glass out to her, clinking it gently with his. 'Here's to us.'

'Mmm,' she said, smiling, and sipped it. 'This is the first time I've drunk champagne in a hay barn.'

He chuckled. 'Me, too. I could grow to like it.'

'Does Florence know?'

'No. I expect my parents have worked it out. They heard us rehearsing the song. And there was champagne in the fridge.'

'Maybe they were expecting to share it with us.'

'They can have some for breakfast,' he said, and taking the glass away from her, he laid her back against the blanket and took her in his arms...

The wedding was planned for the second weekend in September.

They booked a local venue, a hotel and leisure

club that had been refurbished a few years ago and had an excellent reputation, and they'd had a cancellation. They could offer everything—the entire wedding package at a substantial discount.

They didn't care about the discount. What they cared about was that the timing was perfect—and that was dictated as much as anything by the delivery date of the MCMA twins.

'I can't go until they're 32 weeks,' he said. 'If they're still OK then, we'll grab a few days away and I'll make sure Matt's here until we get back, so if anything happens over the weekend, he can deliver them. And we'll have a proper honeymoon later.'

Daisy just smiled at that. She loved him for so many reasons, but his dedication to his patients was definitely one of them, and she was more than happy to fall in with his plans, because she'd become so involved with Mel Grieves and her babies that she wanted to be there when they were born.

She was, but only just.

It was the night before the wedding, and Ben rang her at eleven. Amy was staying with her, and they were still up putting the finishing touches to her headdress when he called.

'One of the twins is struggling. I'm going in with Matt to deliver them.'

'I'm coming!' she yelled, and threw the phone down and ran out of the door, leaping into his car as they pulled away.

'Will we be in time?' she asked desperately, and he shrugged.

'Don't know. Hope so. I can't go any quicker.'

They were in time, Ben on one side, her on the other and Matt standing by, happy to let her play her part. The heartbeats had recovered, but one of the twins had been compromised for a few minutes and she didn't know what they'd find.

Two healthy little girls, was the answer. Very small, but both a good colour, and her eyes filled with tears. Mel had had steroids a few days before, to prepare their lungs, and as they took their first breaths they pinked up beautifully and cried—not loud, not much, but enough that Ben gave a laughing sob as he handed the second one over to the SCBU nurse who was waiting.

Mel was sobbing uncontrollably, so was her husband, and Ben's smiling eyes met Daisy's across the table and he said, 'How's that for a wedding present?'

Wedding! she thought, and glanced up at the clock.

It was ten to twelve, and she looked at him and bit her lip. 'Are you superstitious?'

He glanced at the clock and smiled again. 'Not even slightly, but I'm not doing anything to jinx this marriage. Go home, darling. I'll see you to-morrow.'

'Have a great day,' Mel said, and Daisy stripped off her gloves and hugged her.

'You, too. Congratulations!'

And then she ran.

He was standing there waiting for her, turned towards her with Matt at his side, and even down the length of the crowded room she could see the love in his eyes.

Her father walked her down the aisle between all their family and friends, Florence following behind her with Amy in charge.

Amy, she thought with a flicker of worry, but then she was at Ben's side, and her hand was in his, and she could feel the love radiating from him and warming her heart. 'OK?' he asked softly.

OK? She was marrying the man she loved—the only man she'd ever truly loved. He'd given her so much, taken away the pain and hurt that was her constant companion, and he and Florence had filled her life with love and laughter. It was, quite simply, the best day of her life.

She turned and looked up at him, at the love shining in his eyes, the incredible depth of kindness, the tenderness, the passion. OK?

'Very OK,' she said, and smiled.

* * * * *